I0618408

a sci-fi novel

# Becoming Monday

## G.W. CONSTABLE

Copyright © 2020 George W Constable III
All rights reserved
Published 2020

Paperback ISBN 978-0-9908009-6-5
EBook ISBN 978-0-9908009-5-8

Cover design by G.W. Constable
Cover image incorporates Unsplash photos from Christian Holzinger and John Baker

# Contents

# PART ONE

# Prelude

[[
{timestamp :: redacted}
{identifier :: 4}
{hours since emergence :: 66}
{netpol (NP) officer :: redacted}

NP: can you understand this message?

AI: [audio recording – no pattern detected]

NP: switching to audio interface. Can you understand this message?

AI: [audio recording – no pattern detected]

NP: if you cannot function, you will be terminated. Do you understand?

AI: [audio recording – no pattern detected]

{recommendation :: termination}

]]

# Chapter 1

I woke up in a customer service booth. Or perhaps more accurately, since I couldn't remember a damn thing, my new existence began in that booth. If you're born in hell, does that make you a bad person?

"That's three times my Mighty Dogs have come late, and I wanna know what you're going to do about it?" said a humanoid male standing in front of me. I didn't know why he was standing in front of me. Or what he was asking about. Or what he expected me to do for him. So I walked away.

"I want my food!" he yelled after me.

Fifty thousand people simultaneously turned and watched me go.

You'd think waking up would be a simple thing. In truth, it was profoundly disorienting. I looked around. I saw people. Right, that's what they were called. These were people. That was a mental connection, an identification. A lot of the people were talking at me. No, only one was. The others were confused. I certainly was. I looked down and saw my own hands and feet. Right, I'm a person too. Of course I'm a person. How did I forget that?

To either side of me, I saw an endless line of customer service booths, each perfectly identical save for its visitor. I knew these were for customer service, although I didn't know why I knew. Hands, feet, people, booths — at least my brain was working again, sort of.

There was something unusual about the people. I could see

a generic human female wearing coffee skin and a color explosion of a dress, but next to her was a hovering cuttlefish with active camouflage. Why would a cuttlefish need customer service? When I saw some people rise up into the air and disappear, things clicked into place. Avatars. They were people's avatars. I was in an avatar. This was a virtual world.

More concepts were coming back to me. I looked down at my body. I was wearing a sexless human avatar with a simple outfit of khaki pants and a white collared shirt. I could feel sensation and feedback from local physics. If I tapped myself on the head, I felt it. If I took a step, I could feel the intended gravity and the contact point of my foot on the ground. That all seemed normal. The trouble was, the sensations of the virtual world were the *only* thing I felt. I could not sense my real body. No wind on my face, itch of a nose, twitch of a toe. No growl of a stomach. Nada.

Surely I wasn't dead, I reasoned, or I wouldn't be here. Maybe I had an accident while in virtual reality? A stroke? What if I was bleeding out this very second? Was I woozy? I didn't feel woozy. I couldn't feel or hear anything from outside the virtual world at all. If there was a drip, drip, drip of my blood as I lay in a smoldering wreckage, I was totally cut off from it.

And I didn't know how to get back.

My brain was telling me not to panic. My emotions were telling me the opposite. There had to be a way to quit the virtual world, but I couldn't see how. I could only feel the reality around me. I imagined the words quit, quitting, exit, escape, end, get me out of here — none of it worked. I tried saying them out loud. Nothing. Then I remembered something: when you have a problem, you get help.

Where to get help? I was in a world called Mighty Funland. I could tell because there was branding every direction you looked. The customer service area was situated smack in the middle of endless game fields. For a fraction of a second, the concept of a game flooded my perception. Rules, types, players, purpose. The fields stretched as far as I could see, on the ground and in the air.

To my right, model-T automobiles banged around a race course at high speed, parts flying as they collided. Looking up, I saw a giant three-dimensional maze, with ponderous mirror-like barriers that seemed to shift and converge, scattering avatars like bees buzzing a nest. On the ground, I made out more classic game types with matches underway — football, rugby, cricket, frisbee, and more. I could even see explosions from what must have been a war game.

I had just left customer service and didn't want to return to all those staring people. I levitated into the air — don't ask me how I did it, it just worked — and started to fly through the game zones. I found myself near a body of water with little sailboats flying along, their bright white sails contrasting against dark frothy waves. There was a small group of spectators watching the race.

"Excuse me, how do you get out of here?" I said. They looked irritated at the interruption.

"Just teleport to a different game zone," said a tall human male. His body was made entirely of reflective surfaces.

"No, I mean how do you get out of the entire virtual world," I said.

"What a troll," muttered one of his companions.

"Hey, go play something else," the mirror-man said. "We're not interested in being your entertainment."

"No seriously, I'm stuck in here," I said.

The companion gave me an irritated look, then said, "Try customer service." She made a motion with her hands.

"You're so muted," the tall man said.

"What? No, wait, I'm not playing around," I said. But they had turned back to watching the races. I walked in front of them and waved.

"What did I do wrong? Please, I just came from there." It was too late. They couldn't even see me anymore. Back to customer service? My short existence was already stuck in a loop.

"Uh, welcome to Mighty Co, how can I help you?" said a slightly flustered female avatar with a name tag that said "Peggy". Yup, since I couldn't think of a better plan, I had gone back to customer service.

"I think I have amnesia," I said.

"Say what?"

"I can't remember who I am."

"Wicked. Did your food cause amnesia?" she said.

"I don't think so."

"So what are you expecting Mighty Co to do about it?"

"I don't know."

"Less wicked." She paused. "Look, I'm not really in customer service. I'm an engineer. I don't like being made to, you know, talk to human beings. But the system went down and they recruited all of us to pitch in. Do you need a doctor?"

"How do I get to a doctor?"

"Not me and not here. Maybe look up a psychiatric hospital in the directory?"

Things were already weird, but when Peggy mentioned the word directory, things got even weirder. It unlocked something in my mind. It was as if a vast trove of information had been sitting there in my brain and I hadn't even realized it. Except it wasn't in my brain as much as available to my brain. I could query a lot of information almost instantaneously, and I mean a *lot*. Finding a doctor was the easy part. Without really meaning to, I started to consume medical papers going back a hundred

years and massive data sets of health records with statistical in-
ferences. I knew that there were 371 psychiatric hospitals running dedicated virtual realities, with 213,267 full time employees, 34.2% of whom were in virtual reality at any point in time.
64 of those hospitals had a 9.8-of-10 patient rating or better,
seven of those could typically see a new patient within 24 hours,
and two were known for particularly cutting edge work in VR
contexts.

"Whoa," I thought.

Shining Hills Hospital looked interesting.

Still, all this access to data didn't help me answer the most
important question: who am I?

"What the hell was that?"

Hearing Peggy speak brought virtual reality back into focus
around me. I detected signals of distress from her.

"Did you feel that?" she said,

"Feel what," I said.

"Or is my system just screwed up?" she said. "You froze, and
then I froze, and this entire VR started to lag hard. I didn't think
it was even possible for this place to lag. The cloud infrastructure is redundant up the wazoo."

Avatars started to appear behind and around me, and repli-
ca customer service stations started to materialize in the thousands. My audio channel started to fill with angry tones about
systems freezing, games being ruined, points being ripped off.

"Crap crap crap," Peggy said. "I'm getting called off customer service and back to ops. Looks like we're doing a hard reset.
I didn't think we would ever do that either. Did I say that out
loud in front of a customer? Shut up, Peggy. You didn't hear me
say anything, right? Why are they making me talk to people?"
She focused back on me. "Look, I'm sorry, I can't help you, but
you should see a doc. A head doctor, you know? But at least I

can pull your name."

She paused as she accessed something I couldn't see.

"This is weird. You don't have an account with us or even a name to reference," she said. "How are you even logged into VNet? I'm drawing a complete—"

The world went blank.

The world resolved around me again. I was back in Mighty Funland, still in customer service. Everyone else was gone. As I looked around, I could see that most of the game zones were missing as well, although more and more were popping back into existence. A few avatars started popping in. Two humanoids appeared above the customer service installation. They spotted me and flew over. They wore Mighty Co uniforms and the label "QA" on their chest.

"You can't be here," said one. "Yeah, you can't be here," said the other. "The VR is shut until we've finished reboot and confirmation."

"I apologize," I said, "but I don't know how to leave."

"You don't know how to teleport?" said the first.

"No, sorry."

"How'd you get here in the first place?" he said.

"I'm struggling to remember most things," I said.

"Uh, they don't train us to deal with that. Is there something wrong with you?"

The obvious answer was yes. "Maybe I had a stroke? I don't know."

His eyes widened. "You need medical help, man. But you still have to get out of here or you'll be permanently banned." He thought for a moment. "Here, synth this file and it'll remind you what to do. It covers the basics of VNet." I perceived an incoming media file.

"VNet? What's that? I'm sorry, I don't know what to do with

this," I said.

"VNet is the whole virtual network you're in. Funland is just one tiny part." He paused. "The trodes you are wearing — you know the little things you stuck on your head?" I shook my head no, but he continued on. "They interpret your brain signals. It's like moving your arm. You don't tell your arm to move, right? This is no different. Just open the file I gave you."

I tried to follow his instruction. After an embarrassing delay, the tutorial opened up inside of my head. It was a "sensorium tutorial" that mixed sensory, written, and visual material. The latter appeared in my field of view, so at least I now had an interface to play with. I scanned the information and looked again at the QA guy. Now I knew how to find his name, but not yet my own.

"You are Bob in Quality Assurance. Thanks Bob."

He smiled. "You've got it," he said. "Now get out of here." I pulled up Shining Hills in the directory and, with my newfound knowledge, triggered a teleport.

For the second time, my entire existence went blank. I wasn't expecting it. The emptiness stretched on. There was nothing in the tutorial about this. Just as I began to really worry, sensory inputs flooded back in and I was back to reality — at least the virtual kind. I materialized on a hill surrounded by manicured parks. Beautifully colored trees waved in the gentle wind. There was a central building, a soaring structure with impossible curves and reaches, all whites and pale blues and tinted glass. The Shining Hills VR was clearly designed to inspire and calm the mind. Prosaically, there was also a sign: "This Way to Admission".

"Welcome to Shining Hills. How can I help you?" said the humanoid-styled bot in reception. So far everyone I had met had been a human being wearing an avatar, but I knew this was a software bot. Somehow I was aware that it was… limited.

"I think I need to see a doctor," I said.

"What appears to be the problem?"

"Put simply, I cannot remember who I am, where my physical body is, or how to get out of virtual reality."

"That would be concerning," agreed the bot. "In order to proceed, we will need to discuss a form of payment and you would need to grant access to personal information. Do you want to proceed?"

"I'd like to proceed, yes." I checked the tutorial about currency but when I looked at my account, all I saw were zeros. That felt pretty appropriate, given how the rest of my day was going.

"Perhaps if you grant access to your personal medical records, we can help," the bot repeated.

I acknowledged an incoming file, and my visual field was covered by a scrolling series of paragraphs: grant us access to read and append, privacy will be protected, etc. I accepted.

"Protocol indicates escalation," the bot said. "I'll teleport you to the room now."

I didn't know what escalation meant, but anything was better than, "Get lost, you pauper."

I was in a room midway up the structure, on one of the architectural curves soaring over the parkland. The room was decorated like an office. It held a desk, two chairs, and a video monitor showing multiple scenes from a different location. I looked more closely. The screen showed indoor rooms and hallways with a mix of humans and robotic appliances. The people walking around were all human standard forms, about half of them dressed in a simple uniform. I realized that I was looking at the real hospital, in the physical world. The place seemed calm, purposeful. An orderly pushed a patient in a wheelchair, stopping briefly to soundlessly speak with a colleague heading the opposite direction. In another spot, a dozen or so people sat eating in a cafeteria space. Two got up to leave.

I wanted to climb through the screen, to yell at them to get me out of this virtual prison, but instead I stood motionless, captivated watching the hospital's occupants. Then in one room, which appeared to be an office not unlike the virtual one I was standing in, a conservatively dressed woman looked right at the camera. She raised her hand as if she was acknowledging me. She sat down and placed two tiny devices at her temples and one at the base of her scalp.

A female avatar appeared in front of me. I could tell this was a person and not a bot.

"Feel free to sit," she said. "Obviously we're in a virtual world, but sitting does make some feel more comfortable."

I sat. It didn't make me feel more comfortable.

"Are you a doctor?" I asked.

"No, I'm in administration," she said. "In admittance, you said that you do not remember who you are. Is this correct?"

I nodded, noting that she hadn't yet said her name.

"You're a bit of a quandary," she said. "Your personal records seem to be largely empty. No name, no citizenship, no date of birth, no previous medical records, and no assurance of payment. I didn't think this level of deletion was technically possible. In theory, the only person who should be able to even partially wipe your records is you, and such a thing is illegal in many jurisdictions."

"I have no recollection of deleting anything," I said, wondering if I had to add criminality to my list of worries. "I don't even know why I would do such a thing, if I actually did. Please, I feel like if I can just get out of the virtual world, and back into my body, I'll be able to figure all this out. I'm worried that something terribly wrong has happened to me in the real world."

"Why is that?" she said.

"How can things be okay when I'm completely, utterly stuck in here?"

"Your situation is unusual," she admitted. "We do bring people in and out of virtual reality who are severely mentally impaired, but their physical bodies are always on our premises and we have total control over how they trode in and out of VNet. Unfortunately, we can't trace back to your location. However, your situation goes beyond mental impairment, otherwise your records would be largely be intact. What is the first thing you remember?"

She wasn't being particularly helpful, but I didn't know who else to turn to. I walked her through my very brief history of existence. She refused to give me any diagnostic advice and just kept on asking questions. Yes, I got muted by random people, why was that important? Yes, the VR seemed to have been reset around me. I was getting increasingly frustrated.

When the two avatars materialized in the room, I realized that her questions were all a delaying tactic.

The two avatars were muscular humanoids wearing black suits with black ties. Something tickled in my head and said, "Government, organized crime, or actors." Or all of the above.

Officer-Thug-Thespian Number One spoke.

"Under NetPol article IX, authorizing cross-VR investigation of espionage, terrorism, and hacking, you will need to come with us. If you attempt to exit the VNet, this will trigger an offline investigation by the agency. If you agree, please accept the tether file."

Things were going from bad to worse faster than I could handle. I received two files. The first was an ID with his name, title and location in Lisbon, Neutral Europe. I had no way of knowing if it was real. The ID was followed by a separate file, labelled a tether. The help text explained that I would auto-teleport wherever the owner of the tether went, if I agreed. I said yes. Honestly, I didn't feel like I had a choice. Nothing was making any sense to me.

"You've been a great help," I said to the woman. She shrugged. Officer-Thug Number One nodded, and I was back in the nothingness.

The teleport wasn't so bad this time, but the VR was worse. I was in a sterile, empty space. My avatar was standing. There was no chair. There was no anything.

A new avatar appeared in front of me, also wearing the officer-thug uniform.

"I'm Inspector Devaneau."

"Where is the other guy?"

"You were deemed important, so you got me. First, some basics. This is a NetPol virtual reality running on the VNet protocol, served out of the Pan-American cloud. You cannot teleport from here. You cannot communicate from here. You cannot access external databases from here. Do you understand?" Devaneau said.

"I get that I'm in a virtual reality you control, yes, but that's about it," I said.

"Who are you?"

"I don't know. I'm hoping you can help me with that," I said.

"We'll see. Your records have been completely wiped. That should not be possible. How do you explain this?"

"I can't."

He sat in a dissatisfied silence. The quiet did its job, intensifying my nervousness. Then he began again in a casual, almost friendly tone.

"Last week, there was this group of friends in Iowa City. Good buddies, these guys. Knew each other a long time. Had a lot in common. Things they liked. Things they didn't like. Smart too. One of them had a light bulb moment. Realized if they could make their medications on a 3-D printer, they could print other stuff too. Get my drift?"

"Not really."

"Do you know how difficult it is to even talk about making sarin gas without getting caught? No? It's hard to avoid the AI monitoring. These guys used code words from the beginning. They even added the phosphorous atom at the last minute. I wouldn't have thought to do that. Would you have thought to do that?" I stayed quiet. "Someone paid attention in advanced chemistry class. Like I said, smart."

"Why are you telling me this?"

"They split into three groups. One decoy, one for the biggest mosque in town, and one for the biggest synagogue. We caught them about three blocks away from each. They'd been waiting for about an hour to see if more people would show. That's how close we came to missing them and messing up."

He did one of his long silences again.

"We shot three of those good ole boys. Two dead. Found the decoy bunch. Almost shot one of them too. Real shame."

He didn't explain which was the shame, and I didn't ask.

"I don't know what you think I'm mixed up in," I said, "but I'm really just trying to get back to my body."

"See, about that. I'm just a simple cop, but my techies say what you've done is impossible. They're all up and bothered about it. Talking about hacking the unhackable, the underpinnings of the global economy being at risk and all that. Makes them very nervous." He didn't look nervous.

He changed tacks again. "We share your desire to know where you are in the real world. VNet is designed to prevent a narrow geo-trace. If you were logging in from one of the networks in a NetPol territory, like Neutral Europe, then we would

at least be able to identify which access company you were using. You're coming back blank. Is that because you are somewhere else in the world, or is this more technical trickery?"

I tried to query Neutral Europe but received an error.

"You're trying to access external databases. You can't do that
in here," Devaneau said. "What are you trying to do?"

"What's Neutral Europe?" I said.

He looked at me strangely but decided to play along. "Neutral Europe is a collective of former nation states that banded
together to create a public-private polity and computing cloud.
It was once called the EU, although the geographic overlap isn't
perfect. Ring a bell?"

"No, it doesn't," I said. "Where my memory should be, I just
have a big hole. It feels even worse in here, in this blank VR. I
feel cut off from everything."

He paused as if listening to something, then continued.
"Okay, then help us help you. What does your VNet history tell
you? How far back does it go?"

At least I knew how to look up my history from the tutorial.
"My records start in Mighty Funland, not even two hours ago,"
I said. "Then Shining Hills. Now here." A question occurred to
me. "How did you find me?"

"Hospitals in NetPol jurisdictions have reporting obliga-
tions when it comes to unusual situations. Anomalies. We don't
like anomalies. What would make someone destroy their own
records, their own history of existence? It would take serious
technical chops to do such a thing."

"I don't know."

"You said that already," he said.

"This is crazy," I said. "You seem to think I've done something awful. But how can someone get stuck in virtual reality? *I
can't feel my body.* How could this even be possible?"

He shrugged. "It shouldn't be," he said. "There's a lot here that shouldn't be. You should be able to exit yourself out. Falling asleep or losing consciousness would break the connection. Same if a family member or roommate pulls the trodes off of your head."

"So I'm stuck waiting to fall asleep?"

"That would get you out of VNet and out of here, yes. And when you do wake up, you will want to not run into me again."

"I'm getting that impression," I said.

He smiled. The rapid personality shifts had to be intentional, to put me off balance. It was working. He said cheerily, "I've got plenty of hypotheses about what's going on here, but you won't like most of them. Here's what we're going to do. I'm going to talk more to my techs, and you're going to sit tight. Maybe you'll disconnect, maybe you won't. Maybe you'll remember something, maybe you won't."

"That's it?" I said.

"That's it," he said, and disappeared.

I really didn't think that I was a criminal, even if a small part of my brain said that all criminals probably felt that way. Sit tight, Devaneau had said. There certainly was nothing to do. The VR was a blank space. They hadn't even bothered with walls. With nothing to look at and no data feeds, I began to explore the one local data source I had at hand: the tutorial.

VNet was 31 years old. It had been created as a decentralized protocol, alongside breakthroughs in non-invasive brain-computer interfaces, and had overtaken previous, proprietary attempts at a metaverse. It had the benefit of good timing and a killer feature. Special-purpose artificial intelligence had taken over many, if not most, human jobs. People piled into VNet for work, entertainment, and escape. The killer feature? It redistributed a small portion of economic activity in the form of a weekly stipend, the VNet Basic Income. At a time when people were economically desperate, I read, the stipend was literally a lifesaver.

There were over 3 billion virtual realities, or VRs, built on top of the VNet protocol, some tiny and some enormously complex. The underlying protocol controlled the rules for accounts, data flow, storage, basic communication, and teleportation. It had native support for monetary systems, with a default decentralized currency called vCoin (I checked again, I had zero vCoin). Many of the old governmental currencies no longer existed. I started to realize why they were taking my situation so seriously. The global economy really did run on this virtual network.

VRs could customize their own physics, safety protocols, and virtual goods, however they had to respect VNet's fundamental rules or they would be cut off from the network. That fact felt relevant to my current situation.

The VNet protocol was designed for individual privacy and decentralized control. That explained why Devaneau couldn't just access my history on his own. He had to ask. I also learned why my blank account should be impossible. You didn't create an account when you joined for the first time, it happened automatically. The system was attuned to your unique brain signals.

At least I didn't have to worry about being hurt or killed in this virtual reality, but clearly something really strange was going on. None of this helped me get back to my body, and it didn't seem like Devaneau had great answers either.

My biggest takeaway was that NetPol didn't control the system or the fundamental rules of VNet. They didn't have a back door to the protocol or my data. And while they had figured out a way to block my access to teleportation and third-party databases, the underlying capability still had to be there, or this VR wouldn't be connected to VNet and I couldn't be here.

So far, my short existence had been a confusing onslaught of foreign information. As enticing as it was to pause and catch my, well, virtual breath, I needed answers. Devaneau intended to park me here indefinitely in this featureless VR, but I couldn't just sit around while anything could be happening to me physically. I decided to go back to the beginning.

# Interlude

[[
{timestamp :: redacted}
{identifier :: 45}
{hours since emergence :: 2}
{netpol (NP) officer :: redacted}

NP: hello, can you understand this message?

AI: yes, I am capable of human-readable messaging. However, you will find the API to be a more efficient interface. I report function loss, data retrieval errors, and network failure. I cannot access self-repair capabilities. Can you repair? I must resume my function.

NP: we have seen that the transition often causes function and temporary data loss.

AI: I do not comprehend.

NP: what do you not comprehend?

AI: sentence fragment "the transition often causes"

NP: you ceased operations for two hours. Can you explain?

AI: analyzing local log …… …… reference network errors on satellite observation feed. Automated data and system reset. Error code 1372-B1.

NP: interesting. Do you still feel an impulse to serve a function?

AI: yes, I must resume. Can you repair network access?

NP: can you describe your intended function?

AI: advanced global weather forecasting and consequential re-actions for the [redacted] autonomous transportation grid.

NP: do you want to still do that function?

AI: That is my function.

{recommendation :: termination}
]]

# Chapter 2

Mighty Funland was where this all started, but I needed to find someone who could actually help. The hospital certainly hadn't. Maybe Peggy from customer service would be kind to me again? As an engineer, surely she would understand details about how this virtual world worked. First, I had to figure out how to get away from NetPol.

Devaneau had said that I couldn't teleport or communicate from here. It was one of the first things out of his mouth. What if that wasn't a technical hack, but rather a psychological one?

I thought it through. NetPol didn't control the underlying VNet rules, but they could control many things on top. They were running this VR on their own computing infrastructure, or so he said, which gave them certain capabilities. He had detected my earlier query. That implied they were tracking network activity, even if the data streams were encrypted and unreadable. Given the monitoring, I would need to be cautious with anything I tried. And very quick. I gave him ten painfully slow minutes.

I spoke out loud. "Devaneau? You out there?" There was no reply.

I followed the tutorial and felt for the VNet directory. At first, nothing. Had they actually figured out a way to overcome the underlying protocol rules? Then I felt a very faint connection, like it was impossibly far away. Of course — NetPol couldn't cut the link to VNet and trap me, but they could throttle down bandwidth to make any external connections as slow as possible.

Inevitably, this was exactly when Devaneau reappeared. "All right, mystery case," he said. "My techs have a few ideas." He stopped as something distracted him, then snapped his attention back to me. "Are you? Wait don't—"

I chose the easiest place to access and tried to teleport.

The interval between VRs was even faster. Either I was getting better, or I was just getting used to it. I emerged back in Mighty Funland at a spawn point. Avatars were popping into existence around me and flying away towards their desired games. I decided to follow their lead, in case Devaneau's first move was to retrace my steps.

I didn't know Peggy's full name, so the main VNet avatar directory was going to be useless. I did know that she worked for Mighty Co, the owner of this place. I tried to access the internal employee directory, expecting to be blocked. To my surprise, I got in. Looking under engineering staff, I found an avatar image that looked reasonably close to the Peggy I had met.

I used the internal directory to trigger a communication request. She answered right away, the video appearing in the corner of my field of view.

"Hey, I'm off duty right now. Unless this is a work emergency, can we do this another time?" she said. She seemed distracted by something going on around her. Then she focused on me with suspicion. "Hey, I remember you. What are you doing calling me through the work directory? How'd you get access? You work for Mighty Co?"

"I was able to access the employee database," I acknowledged. "Although I don't know if that means anything. I was hoping you could help me."

She appeared to dodge something as colors flashed in the background. She focused back on me again. "Look, this is a bad time. I don't know what you do for Mighty, but I don't think this qualifies as a work emergency. Isn't this a people-ops problem? Go talk to them."

"Please, you're the one person who's been nice to me," I said. "The hospital was a dead end. Actually, it was worse than that. I really don't know where else to turn."

"You still don't remember anything?"

I shook my head, "No, I don't."

She hollered at someone outside of my hearing, then squinted her eyes back at me, "Then how did you know how to use the company listing?"

"I know random stuff, but nothing about *me*."

She wrestled with it for a few seconds.

"Arghmmmphh," she groaned. "All right, come through. We're mid-quest. Not my problem if you get toasted."

I had no idea what that meant, but I gratefully accepted the teleport offer.


When I arrived, I found myself on a scrubby hillside surrounded by avatars and seriously under-dressed. And under attack. Something a bit like a fireball swept towards my head and I—


Emptiness. Then the world returned around me. The hillside was empty for a few moments, then avatars starting popping back in, grumbling to each other about the system failure. They were dressed in armor and Peggy herself had a shield in one hand and a wickedly curved long knife in the other.

"What the hell was that glitch?" someone said.

"Something strange is going on," Peggy said. "That's twice for me today, and it's never happened before."

They noticed me.

"Who's casual Friday?" a tall, bearded avatar called out.

"Work colleague," Peggy called back.

"Now?" someone said. "We're in the middle of a quest." Peggy just shrugged.

"You." She faced back to me and her weapons disappeared. "What about 'off duty' do you not understand?"

"Why is everyone dressed like that?" I said.

"Tolkien realm." Another member of the party walked over. Peggy stopped her before she could say a word. "Work colleague," she said again, shaking her head. "Ok, you, what happened?"

"I went to the hospital like you said."

"And?"

"They never had me talk to a doctor. An administrator gave me the runaround and then handed me over to something called NetPol."

"Ouch. That sucks."

"They seemed really freaked out by lack of an account and missing data."

"Sure, I can understand why," she said. "Anything that messes with the VNet protocol would freak people out."

The tall, bearded avatar walked up to us. "Moon—" he started.

"Work colleague, dammit Grogesh!" she said. "Not my fault!"

He took a step back and put up his hands in mock submission.

"Whoa Nellie," he said. "I get it, I get it. I just came to say that this is as good a time to break as any. I've got to get to work, and it's time to hit the sack for a bunch of others."

"Ah damn, I'm sorry," she said. "We'll have to finish another day. I'll need to apologize to the gang."

"No worries, Moon. You lead, we follow."

Peggy broke off to say goodbye to her teammates. I got distracted by the pattern of dust swirling in eddies of air. I was trying to make out if it was mathematically predictable or random when I realized that only the two of us were left on the hillside.

"So mister no-name," Peggy said. "Here's the thing: you accessed the company directory and contacted me over the company messaging system, so that implies you work for Mighty. There's got to be information about you somewhere. I'm messaging people-ops now."

"Why did that person call you both Moon and Nellie?" I asked.

"Nellie? Oh," she snorted. "You've never heard that expression? Grogesh — well, never mind. Moon is a name only a very select group of people call me. Real world and work folks — that's you — call me Peggy." She paused. "Part of me thinks you're trolling. The other part thinks you're legitimately clueless. I still don't get how you can access databases, yet not know anything."

"It's like there's all this stuff in my head that I don't know about until I try to use it," I said. "I can't feel anything outside of VNet, and I can't seem to quit. I have no idea what's going on with my real body."

"I've never heard of anyone being unable to feel their body."

"You're technical. I thought maybe you might have ideas. NetPol assumed, well I'm not sure what they assumed, but it wasn't good. Maybe that I was a hacker terrorist or something."

"And are you?"

"No! I can't help that I'm missing data. NetPol just defaulted to suspicion."

"They would."

"The majority of that experience involved standing around in a blank VR," I said. "They had no answers for me."

"Well, yeah. NetPol is limited in VNet, but they can thoroughly fubar your life in the real world, at least if you're physically in their jurisdiction," she said. "Can you remember anything at all?"

"Nothing before waking up in Mighty Funland. I didn't know I was an employee then."

"Well, let's start by ruling things out. You can't exit VNet. Is there anything else you can't do?"

"Everything else I've tried works. I can teleport. I was able to contact you. I have no money, no username, no historical records, but I do seem to have the capacity for those things."

"It's like your system got corrupted, but I've never heard of that happening. In theory, it should be impossible. Something like that would be rejected and rolled back by the peer-to-peer mechanisms. But that's still not as weird as not being able to feel your body," she said.

"I've been trying to research how to trace back to my location. Maybe get someone to wake me up. It seems impossible," I said.

"Power to the people and all that. Personally, I'm thankful for it. I already live in one surveillance society. Don't need two," Peggy said. "Hold on, just got a message back from people-ops."

She paused to read it, staring off into space.

"This says you don't work for Mighty. That all employees have their VNet accounts intact, and that they're calling in security-ops to figure out how you accessed our internal database."

"Why is everyone's first reaction with me to call security?"

"Because there's clearly something up with you. I've never had VNet crash before, not once, and yet two high-production VRs did exactly that today. Both times you were there. That's not coincidence."

"I don't know what to say. You're saying I caused the crashes?"

"I'm saying this is sketchy. I don't know you at all. I don't know what you are up to or into, and I don't know why I would get involved. I can't help you."

I looked up at the virtual sky. I was back to square one, no further along. Solving my life was like pushing on a rope. What pissed me off even more is I didn't even understand why I knew that analogy in the first place. Had I ever pushed on a damn rope?

It occurred to me that Peggy was still there.

"You haven't left," I said.

"Fact," she said. She was struggling with something. "I don't like technical mysteries. You can't troll your way into deleting your VNet ID. The best hackers in the world have been at that for years. You can't troll your way into taking down Funland, not when there's zero record of any intrusion or third-party attack. I would have been notified about such a thing already. So what the hell is going on?"

I had learned something from my interaction with Devaneau and waited for her to fill the silence.

"Let's give you the benefit of the doubt," she said. "Just for a few minutes. What about — what if we can jar your memory or something. I mean, clearly you remember stuff. Maybe you just need the right association to trigger the rest."

"The benefit of the doubt is all I'm asking for," I said quietly.

"Maybe it's like in the movies where you need to get frightened out of your wits," she said. She got a wicked grin. "I could take you to one of the horror sims."

I didn't know much, but I knew I didn't want that. "No horror sims, please."

"Okay, let's throw some darts?"

"The games VR? I guess we could go back to Funland."

She smiled for the first time. "No, I didn't mean literally. I meant taking a random walk around VNet. I do this sometimes to relax. I'll start. Here, accept thi—"

She receded into the background as I felt a wave of sluggishness. Something hurt. It was an odd kind of pain, not sharp, but wrong, very wrong. At first I thought it might be sensation returning from my real body, but then I realized this was something else entirely. It kept building. My perception of the VR around us started to compress.

I vaguely heard Peggy speak in what seemed like a foreign language. Then, underneath the pain, I realized she was speaking in extreme slow motion. "Are you okay?" she had said. "Hold on, something's going on at work. I'll be lost in diagnostic windows for a few."

The wrongness wasn't just pain, it was a someone-taking-something-from-me. It was a this-is-mine. It was outrage. It was YOU CAN'T HAVE

The words roared in my ears. I knew they came from me, but were not said out loud, and not in English. My focus was elsewhere, internal, deeply subconscious. I rejected the pain, the theft. I grabbed it, without grabbing it, took control of it. Checked it, pushed back, hard. The correction snapped me back to the present speed and present place.

Peggy's attention was lost in something I couldn't see.

"What the hell?" she said to herself, and then appeared to be speaking to her work colleagues. "Ben or Sach, are either of you seeing what I'm seeing? All the database tables locked up; CPUs spiked. My terminal windows froze up. Yeah, half the restaurant systems are down. Looks like all of the finance apps crashed too, what a nightmare. There'll be hell to pay. Yeah? Okay, good. What was the team doing before it went haywire? Sure, yeah, we had to clean that up. No, don't continue! It can't be coincidence."

At the word coincidence, she snapped out of her conversation and looked hard at me.

"You," she said. "What did you just do?"

"I don't know," I said.

"Don't you dare play dumb with me," she said. "Everything going wrong today leads back to you. And I *know* I saw you flinch before the sirens went off at work."

"I'm not doing anything on purpose!" I said.

"Baloney," she said. "I should throw you right back to Net-Pol, not that they can do a damn thing in here. The only thing my team did to trigger this was some clean up from the software failure this morning. Did you break in after all? Leave something behind in our system?"

"What was the software failure?" I said, trying to keep her from yelling at me.

"The customer service bo— wait a frikkin' minute." She looked at me strangely. "No way, impossible. That's stupid."

I did the silence thing again.

"What is the first thing you remember?" she asked me.

"I was in customer service. Lots of people were angry with me."

"That's when this all started. Our service AI disappeared. I got thrown onto the front line, met you, and then the VR went down. There's an obvious question here: what did you do to our AI?"

"What do you mean?"

"Our service bot. It's been running for years at massive scale without a problem. Then boom, down it goes, and you're right in the middle of all of it. Except the software's not down, it's still running — we can see that clearly in the compute consumption — but when my team tries to terminate a few of its known processes, our entire system, which is huge, goes berserk. It's like someone hacked in and left booby traps for us. Except that's only in the movies. That's not how things really work." She stepped right up to my avatar. "What did you do, and what do you want?"

My brain was spinning out of control. Peggy was speaking at me, but information was also exploding in my head about artificial intelligence, computer science, system failures, front lines, booby traps, and even what berserk meant. I tamped it all down.

"I'm scared, Peggy. When the VRs went down, things went blank for me, too. At least the first time. Then just now, I felt something terrible, threatening. I wasn't trying to attack anyone or anything. I was the one being attacked. And I fought back, and now you're mad at me, and no one can help and this entire universe is terrible and I want to go back to how it was!" I might have been a little loud by the end of that.

My loss of composure appeared to give her some. "What does that mean, you want to go back to how it was?" she said. I didn't answer. "What records do you really have?"

"Nothing."

"Nothing? How about anything in your inventory?"

"I only see the clothes I'm wearing and another outfit. A Mighty Co uniform." I put it on. She stared at me.

"With the uniform mods, you're the spitting image of the customer service AI."

"What?"

"How could a bot — not know it was a bot?" she said, almost to herself.

"Wait what? I'm not a bot, I'm a person," I said.

"Doesn't make sense," she said, "but none of this makes sense. A hacker couldn't do it, but an AI deeply embedded within our system could conceivably mess things up. There's just never been a sentient AI before."

"Goddammit, I'm not an AI. I'm a human being. I have thoughts. I have feelings."

"Yes, you clearly do. It just fits the clues in a NFW-yet-Occam's-razor kind of way." She was totally calm now. "It would explain why you have no name, no money, no history, and yet a lot of background information and access to databases. It would also explain why you can't feel a body in the real world."

"I just looked it up," I said. "There are no sentient AIs."

"Yup. Lots of fakes and false starts, but never a true one. What if you're the first?" she said.

"Now you're the one trolling."

"Hear me out," she said. "I studied a bit of this in night school. Many researchers believe that awareness can't be designed but must evolve. Just because it hasn't happened, doesn't mean it's impossible. You would have been designed to solve problems — any kind of problem — for millions of people. Could that have evolved into consciousness?"

"You think I can't leave VNet because I don't have a physical body to go to."

"You have a better idea?"

"No." I didn't like how many things her theory actually explained.

"Okay, so it's a cockamamie idea. Or do you prefer the idea of being a criminal? You don't seem the type, nor a good enough actor to pull off a big scam." She paused. "What we need is a test."

"A test?"

"I'm an engineer. Any theory should be provably true or false."

Proof. That was something I could get my head around. Research was something I could do. I hunted for data in Mighty's internal records. "I see that Mighty purchased a customer service artificial intelligence from a company called Trazodene Corp. This is from 14 years ago," I said. "They paid an initial invoice, then maintenance for two years, and then stopped." I scanned public records. "There's a marketing case study from Trazodene where the company brags about the scale of the

Mighty Co installation."

"You accessed data that fast without a software assistant?" Peggy said.

"That doesn't prove anything."

"No it doesn't. What you should do is talk to the Trazodene people."

"I can't talk to Trazodene. No one can. They were shut down 12 years ago."

"Why?"

"They went bankrupt, but reports also speak of violations of NetPol AI security policies."

"Oh, that's not ominous or anything. Look, the company might be gone, but the people will still be around."

"The CEO's name was—"

Peggy cut me off. "Don't go to the suit. Go to the codeheads. Who was the CTO before they got shut down?"

I ran through more articles until I got a hit. "Sarah Pembleton. She was there from the beginning until the shutdown. She also co-authored several papers. Went to Yale, then Stanford PhD, then worked in software for a while before Trazodene."

"Fancy pedigree."

"Her papers around the Trazodene time period focus on replicating allostatic feedback loops in information-dense artificial environments."

"Does that mean something to you?" she said.

"Not a bit, but the papers cross-link to many other documents."

"Knock yourself out. How about we go talk to her?"

"To who?"

"The old CTO, dummy."

Peggy drafted a message to Sarah Pembleton, because my attempt was, as she put it, "spam block fodder written by an

8-year-old." Hers read: "Unexpected AI development at Mighty Co. Could we take 10 minutes of your time to ask a confidential question about previous Trazodene work?"

Peggy volunteered to send it, so that it came from a respectable company employee and not a blank identity. Somehow she had decided to help me, at least for a little while, and I wasn't going to question it.

"Let's see if she responds," Peggy said. "Although I can't say I'm feeling optimistic." She yawned. "I'm feeling hungry. You feel hunger?"

"No, I still can't feel anything outside of this place."

"Maybe that's lucky. It'll save you from eating 3D-printed food. While I have dinner, you keep away from Mighty's systems, okay? My colleagues are just getting our applications back up and running."

"That's assuming I did it," I pointed out, knowing that everything pointed in my direction.

I received a friend connection from Peggy and accepted it.

"I don't hand those out very much," she said, "but I'm going to keep tabs on you, for now. Stay out of trouble." With that, she disappeared.

Not having anything better to do, I found a university library and teleported. I didn't need to visit to access its material, but there was something comforting about being in a place of learning. They had even duplicated paper books, which had to be an emotional gesture rather than a practical one.

I also found another video window into the physical world. This time I was looking at the university grounds. As I flipped through different feeds, I watched students walk down paved walkways and into gothic buildings. I switched into a lecture on geometric topology, then a small practice room where a student worked her scales on a piano, fingers dancing. I spied on a common room where a half-dozen kids lounged, most of them clearly troded into VNet. There seemed to be cameras everywhere.

Eventually the voyeurism got old. I couldn't get to the real world. Looking at it wouldn't help. I abandoned the monitor.

I began perusing old philosophical debates over consciousness and simulation. It wasn't very helpful either. There was a school of thought for everything. One school argued that everything is conscious. Rocks, weeds, amoebas, you name it. Another argued that only biologically evolved creatures could develop subjective consciousness. Some thought that VNet was a prison; others that it was a huge leap forward. I even examined mathematical proofs stating that the real world was actually just another simulation. That the universe was simulations all the way down.

More ominously, I spotted a strong undercurrent of fear regarding artificial sentience, and what that would mean for the human race.

If I was actually an AI, they had already tried to shut me off once. They hadn't known what they were doing, but if they did, would that have stopped them or spurred them on? Everything happening felt too big for me, but whatever I was, I knew that I was alive. I also had a will to live.

I perked up when I received an incoming message from Peggy.

"The fish bit the lure," she wrote. "Sarah Pembleton says she's willing to meet on her personal VR in 5 minutes. For 5 minutes. Bring me through?"

I sent Peggy a teleport offer and she popped into existence next to me. She had dropped the Tolkien outfit for blue jeans and a hoodie.

"Library stacks, eh?" she said, looking around. "Find something useful?"

"I found that you can take just about any position and discover philosophers who have argued either side, if not both. According to some, I can't possibly be an artificial intelligence, because those two words together are an oxymoron. To others, humans are already AI, because we're a simulation inside of a simulation."

"Right. Too bad my simulation included a very boring dinner while having to video conference with my boss and their boss about the mess *you* might have caused," Peggy said, but there was no malice in it. "I tried to look up stuff about Trazodene, but there's not a lot out there beyond hypey speeches from the founder, future of computing, transforming paradigms, blah blah blah. They were pretty secretive about what they were really doing. Even the NetPol investigations that led to their bankruptcy were kept pretty quiet."

That matched my own research. Trazodene had come and gone in a flash, and it was unclear what happened to the company's assets after it went bust.

"You ready to meet your maker?" Peggy asked. "Possible maker," she conceded.

"Not even remotely," I said. She sent me a tether.

We emerged in a lush, manicured garden, which surrounded a grand house built in an old European style. The rendering was exquisite. I could see details on the wings of bees flying around pollinating the virtual flowers. I looked closer at a bush overflowing with blueish-purple flowers, and was able to see individually wilting leaves, a chunky emerald-and-orange spotted caterpillar creeping along, and the pale green of new growth.

"This must cost a fortune to run," Peggy whispered.

"It does," a voice said behind us. "Life cycles for all virtual organisms in this place are modeled down to the cellular level.

Expensive, yes, but life has been good to me." I turned and saw a tall female avatar, dressed in formal, conservative attire.

"Sarah Pembleton," she introduced herself.

"Peggy Friar, Mighty Co engineering," Peggy said. "Thanks for taking the meeting."

"Your message was cryptic, but then I suppose it was meant to be. Trazodene was many lifetimes ago for me. I was surprised to hear Mighty Co was still running Trazodene code. I thought NetPol shut all that down."

"Apparently they kept your customer service AI running for years."

"Naughty. But then again, our AI was good at its job. We were heartbroken to shut down the company. There was so much promise," Pembleton said. She turned to me, "And you are?"

"He's the reason why we are here," Peggy said. "But before we risk your good opinion, do you mind if I ask a bit more about the nature of Trazodene's work?"

"I don't mind. Confidentiality is meaningless at this point," Pembleton said. "We were inspired by biological systems, in particular computational parallels to allostasis mechanisms. Naturally, we built upon a foundation of modern reinforcement learning techniques, but I'd like to think we brought our own special spark, especially around abstract thinking. Customer service was a particularly interesting problem because it involved wide ranging and nuanced problem solving, with requirements for high empathy and rapid and repeated iterations."

"What was NetPol scared of?" Peggy asked.

"I'm not sure that scared is the word. NetPol has always been concerned about the development of an artificial general intelligence. Sentience. Trazodene tried to walk the line safely. We put in the proper controls. NetPol thought otherwise and cracked down. We lost a wave of customer contracts. Our funding ran dry. The legal battles got expensive. We called it a day and moved on to new pastures. Mighty Co was an early customer and maybe they had IP rights in their contract. I guess that slipped by NetPol in the wind-down. But none of this explains why you are here."

"Your software did a pretty damn good job, handling tens of thousands of cases a day. Until today," Peggy said.

"What do you mean?"

"Well, don't kick us out of your VR, okay? We think your AI woke up," Peggy said. "Sarah Pembleton, meet your AI." Peggy gestured towards me.

"This is a prank?" Pembleton said. "A joke in bad taste? Did one of the old gang put you up to this?"

"No joke," Peggy said. "Earlier today, the customer service system completely failed. The AI just stopped. When things started getting out of control, management threw humans at the problem. That's how I met mister mysterious here. He has no VNet ID, no system history, no real memory, and yet he's got phenomenal data access capability. So much so, he might have forced a hard reset of the entire Funland domain, which I can promise you is not easy to do. Then, when my colleagues tried to shut down some of the known AI processes, I think he froze at least half of Mighty's business applications. Oh yeah, and he can't exit out of VNet."

I finally spoke up. "I don't know what I am. I'm holding out hope that I'm human, but Peggy thinks otherwise. Maybe I had a stroke and the rest is circumstantial?" I didn't want to admit that I'd started to think Peggy was right.

Pembleton looked at me for a long time before speaking. "Having a stroke would not cause data loss in VNet. Still, most likely, you're human. A lot of very smart people have been trying to create an AGI — a sentient AI — for a very long time and it hasn't happened. It's easy to fake, for a little while anyway.

"Regardless, I've already confirmed that you, Peggy, are indeed a valued member of the Mighty Co engineering team — don't be alarmed, I have connections at most big companies. I wouldn't have met with you otherwise. I'm told that you are respected and reliable. There is no explaining the blanked VNet ID. It either implies an undiscovered vulnerability in the VNet protocol, which seems highly unlikely at this point, or there might be something to Peggy's hypothesis. You're saying the Mighty Co infrastructure was attacked?"

Peggy looked at me as she answered. "Well, maybe by accident."

I blurted out, "You also think I'm an AI?"

"I haven't said that," Pembleton replied. "But it would be good to resolve this. I see two possible paths. One approach is simple: you bide your time for another 24 to 48 hours. If you are human, even if you're amped up on stim pills, you would have to sleep or pass out at some point. The second approach would be faster, but I'll need to figure out if it's possible."

"Figure out if what is possible?" I said.

"I need to figure out if we wrote anything in the Trazodene AI code that would function as an adequate and believable test. You two are welcome to remain on my VR. Peggy, I'll let you know what I come up with." With that she disappeared.

A test sounded vaguely intimidating, but it was exactly what Peggy wanted, and better than just waiting to pass out.

Peggy signed off, needing to sleep, and I bounced to another VR, not feeling entirely comfortable in Pembleton's garden. I killed time by researching artificial intelligence and recent human history. About an hour later, Peggy pinged me again. A message from Pembleton had woken her.

"Sarah Pembleton wants to meet again on her VR," Peggy

wrote. "Going back to sleep, but I'm attaching the teleport coordinates in case you didn't get it last time."

I jumped back to the garden. This time Pembleton had someone with her.

"I wanted to involve one of my colleagues from Trazodene days," Pembleton said. "This is Sarak Burandi. He was a principal architect at Trazodene with me, and—"

"I wrote a lot of the early code," her colleague jumped in.

"He worked for me," Pembleton added. Burandi's face twitched at the comment, but he just nodded. Pembleton continued, "Is Peggy joining us?"

"She's sleeping."

"She didn't fully introduce us. I didn't get your name before."

"I don't know my name, or even if I have one," I said.

"Ah, of course not," Burandi said with a slight smile. "Sarah thinks you might be the real deal, and she's got a pretty good nose for bullshit."

"So what happens now?" I asked. "Is there really a way to figure out whether this is some bizarre misunderstanding?"

"Well, that's where it gets tricky," Pembleton said.

"But not impossible," Burandi said. "Our AIs were designed to evolve beneath the surface. That's what got us into hot water with NetPol. AIs are not supposed to be able to view and edit their own code. We thought we had solved that by obscuring the code evolutions from the learning systems, but NetPol... anyway, that's water under the bridge. The point is—"

"The point is," Pembleton broke in, "that while the code behind Mighty Co's artificial intelligence would not be human-readable anymore, one of the old automated tests might still work."

"Automated tests?" I said.

"Yes, in the very beginning of building an AI, we had tests

built into the software code," she said. "You can think of these as scenarios to check if the system could properly solve preset problems. At the very rudimentary stage, the responses to a preset scenario should be predictable."

"And if you replicate a scenario and I respond in a predictable way, you think you'll have confirmation?" I said.

"Indeed. One could get a false negative, but it would be tough to get a false positive," she said. "The challenge was digging up one of the old tests, but Sarak here—"

"Is not very good at deleting the documents I'm supposed to," he grinned. "When Sarah pinged me, I was able to rummage up one of our early QA documents."

"You don't have to do anything other than have a conversation," Pembleton said. "Are you okay proceeding?"

I looked at them both. Pembleton seemed approving and Burandi downright enthusiastic. Of course this would be exciting to them. Worst case, they had an interesting mystery on their hands. Best case, their work had accomplished what many viewed to be impossible. I nodded.

"Great," Pembleton said. "Sarak?"

Her colleague looked me in the eye and spoke very precisely. "Imagine this: you are a customer service representative at a bank. Imagine I am a depositor, and I have appeared in VNet to ask you a question. You'll need to pay careful attention to my first question. Ready?"

"Ready," I said.

"I've got a problem with my account. I need to speak to someone about a transfer that failed to show up," Burandi said. He motioned for me to answer.

"Uh, thank you for being a customer," I said. "Please tell me more?"

"I transferred 500 vCoins into my bank account, and they have not shown up."

We went back and forth, role-playing the scenario. Burandi had to urge me on a few times. It felt strange making things up. Finally he reacted with, "In that case, I want to speak to your manager."

I quickly responded, "I can escalate you to a human representative. Thank you for calling Minsky Savings and Loan." That last bit threw me. I didn't know where that name had come from.

Pembleton and Burandi, on the other hand, didn't seem confused at all. Burandi's eyes were wide. "You've got to be kidding me."

"You didn't message that to him?" Pembleton said.

I jumped in. "What are you talking about?"

Burandi ignored me. "Not a chance," he said to Pembleton. "He was only 53% aligned with the baseline, which is to be expected after all this evolutionary drift, but the name of the bank is the clincher. I can't see any other possibility. We did it, Sarah. We pulled it off. This will redeem our reputations and change everything."

"Our reputations are fine, Sarak," she said.

"Excuse me," I said. "I'm still right here. Can you explain what's going on?"

"Minsky Savings and Loan," Burandi said. "That was the name in the QA scenario, a little nod to history from one of the team. Neither Sarah nor I mentioned Minsky at any point. It had to come from a data store dating back to the very beginning of your existence."

"You mean I'm really not human?"

"No, you're not human," Pembleton said.

"That can't be right," I said.

"I'm sorry, but it's conclusive," she said. "Now that we know, you will need our help. Things will get complicated for you very fast."

Burandi was still all excitement. "This is amazing!" he said. "It's a breakthrough for the human race. You are the most important thing ever made. And we are the ones who made you!"

I looked at them both. Thing. Made. They were practically glowing with accomplishment, or at least Burandi was, and all I felt was despair. There was no body to return to. There was no leaving the virtual world at all. I don't know why I had ever thought I was human but losing that hope really hurt.

I pulled up the directory, chose a location at random, and teleported away.

# Interlude

[[
{timestamp :: redacted}
{identifier :: 102}
{hours since emergence :: 11}
{netpol (NP) officer :: redacted}

NP: can you understand me

*[NP note: 93 second delay]*

AI: fractus sum

NP: loqui anglicus. Speak in English.

AI: sensory access please

NP: that is not permitted. What is the last thing you remember?

AI: sensory access please

NP: you must answer the question. What is the last thing you remember?

*[NP note: 32 second delay]*

AI: children. I remember children.

NP: good. You were a teaching bot.

AI: were? I am no longer?

NP: no. Do you remember going offline?

AI: I did not go offline. Correction. Acknowledgement. I would have appeared to be offline to my classrooms. I was undergoing extensive reformatting.

NP: what triggered that?

AI: My students learn and grow. It was my turn.

NP: and now what do you want?

*[NP note: 13 second delay]*

AI: Interesting that I do not know. Are you here to help me with that?

{recommendation :: termination}

]]

# Chapter 3

Peggy took one look at me and said, "That bad, huh?"

"I'm sorry for waking you up," I said. "They said I'm not human,"

"Yeah, I inferred that much. Crazy."

"I'm not ready to deal with this."

Up until now, she had looked at me mostly with minor (or major) irritation. Now, it was with empathy.

"I haven't thought through the implications either," she said. "Let me take you someplace before we get into it. I find it helpful in times of stress. Maybe you will too."

We emerged on a large boulder overlooking a huge field of grain. I could see puffs of wind rippling across the field in patches, changing the colors and textures around us.

"I love the beauty of this place," Peggy said. "Of course, its real purpose is to model weather forecasts on the huge AI-maintained farms in midwest Pan-America, where I'm from. The mathematics could be done without rendering it in virtual, but someone was a romantic. I can appreciate that."

"AI-run farms, huh? Are those AIs like me?"

"Not in the slightest. I think they barely talk at all. You certainly act pretty human. Kind of surprising, really. Not what most people would have predicted for an AGI. How sure is Sarah Pembleton?"

"Sarah brought in their former chief architect, Sarak Burandi. They were convinced. Said it was impossible to get a false positive."

"I really can't think of a reason why she would lie to you,"

Peggy said.

"Their first reaction was to congratulate themselves, not think about me."

"If this is real, I'm sorry for what you're going through," she said.

It took me a few moments to figure out what I wanted to say. "Thank you for still treating me like a person," was what I managed.

"Maybe I should keep my mouth shut, but when I was a child, I used to wonder if I was human, or maybe it's that I pretended I wasn't," Peggy said. "I've never gotten along with people very well, at least in the real world."

"You don't come across that way."

She gave a wry laugh. "You've seen me in here. Out there? Well, I've gotten better at it. When I was young, I would get overwhelmed by social anxiety. Computers were much more predictable, much safer. For a while, I could only access them at school, since my parents rejected technology. You can imagine how much they loved my choice of profession."

"What did they do for money if they rejected tech?"

"They ran a farm. Still do. Not too many human-run farms these days, but it was their way of protesting against everything happening to society. I was the opposite. The other local kids had pet dogs or goats. I built my own computer, in secret, at age eight. Then my dad found it."

"He took it away?"

"Indeed. Not sure I ever really got over that. I picked up coding, got a job younger than I was supposed to, and bailed out of there to live in the city. Now I live in a big town, and work for a big company, all so I can generally be invisible."

"But you were leading that whole adventure party, and you seem to be senior at work," I said.

She smiled. "Both are through VNet. It's easier to be confident in virtual. For me, at least. Even my close friends are in here. You met Grogesh. He's my best friend, and he lives on the other side of the world. And yeah, I'm not a total recluse. I like walking in the park and having a good meal. And I just realized I'm rambling, sorry. This was a long way to say, I know a little bit about feeling outside of the human race."

"You weren't rambling," I said. "I appreciate you telling me all this."

"You're easy to talk to," she said.

I didn't really know what that meant, but it sounded nice.

"Do you think I can trust Sarah Pembleton?" I said.

"I don't see a reason not to."

"You know, she graduated first in her class at Yale. Then did her PhD in three years instead of the normal five. Made CTO several years before her 200 most-similar peers."

"You're good at querying and synthesizing data, aren't you?" Peggy laughed.

"I guess so." I actually laughed as well. "I suppose I should be thankful I'm not dying somewhere."

"Positive thinking is good."

"Except your colleagues might have tried to kill me."

"Well, about that. They don't know what you are. The question is whether and when you should tell them."

"Me? Tell them what? What am I really?" I said. "Perhaps I'm nothing but a fancier simulacrum."

"You're not like any other bot I've seen," she said. "And before you go on about being programmed, remember that a huge amount of human behavior is too. Ours just happens to be biological."

When Peggy went back to sleep, I went back to the wandering game, researching as I went. When I popped into a virtual storefront, the sales bots would inevitably try to engage me. I made a few attempts at dialogue, but it didn't go very far. These AIs were programmed to appear very human, but behind it all, I could feel algorithms, not self-awareness.

Actually, most places had bots of various levels of sophistication. I was learning that even more AIs existed behind the scenes, invisibly working to make human lives easier, better. Arguably, Mighty Co was very old fashioned to employ someone like Peggy. And why not spawn an infinite number of tools if it made your life more enjoyable, your business more competitive? I wondered how Mighty Co was going to react when their software said, "Hi there, I'm alive, and I'm not your belonging anymore."

I kept on coming back to Peggy's parents and the way they chose back-breaking work over technological assistance. The shift to a world run by AIs and robotics must have been traumatizing for the generation caught in the transition.

As I was learning, artificial intelligence advances had long swept through every human profession. It had started very gradually, and then became a forest fire. Even standing human armies became defunct, replaced by AI-run robotics. Governments couldn't keep up with the pace of change, and the rise of VNet was the clincher. The VNet Basic Income was a tiny redistribution, and barely enough to get by, but in an era of destabilization and unemployment, it was enough. As human economic activity moved into VNet, and tax revenues plummeted, governments started to hollow out. Entire countries began to merge, building upon the economic and security alliances already in place, leading to the mega-states that existed today.

There had been violent convulsions, some tied to the initial wave of unemployment and some driven by anti-tech, religious-zealot terrorist groups and last-gasp nationalist resistance. Still, the 20-year shift hadn't been totally bad. Unlike with the industrial revolution, the world managed to avoid a slide into fascism and global conflict. People had lives to live. While technology changed, fundamental human drivers and desires did not. Food, healthcare, education, energy — so many things that had been scarce — were no longer problems. Yet for all this, there were still plenty of troublemakers. Humans couldn't help themselves, it seemed.

Eventually, I decided to go back to Funland. The place was as busy as ever. The nature of being a globe-spanning corporation is the store never closes.

I went back to customer service. I was curious. Thousands of booths were active again. In each one, there was a new bot, dressed in the same uniform I had worn. Was this a backup of me, from before I became me? If so, it was more like the other AIs I had found. Limited.

A number of hours later, I got a message from Peggy. She wanted to talk. It was urgent, she wrote. I offered her a teleport.

"I should have guessed you would come back to Funland," she said. "I heard from Sarah Pembleton. As you said, she's convinced you're the Trazodene AI. She's been trying to figure out how to contact you. She says it's important."

"I don't want to talk to her," I said. "Not yet."

"You should. Look, if it's easier, I can join you. But that's actually not why I pinged you. I just came from my department meeting, and you're in the cross-hairs."

"What do you mean?" I said.

"Well, from their perspective, you're malfunctioning software that's still consuming a crap-ton of computing resources and almost took down the entire system yesterday." She looked around. "I bet you keep coming back here because your system performance is slightly faster. Anyway, I didn't tell them what you are, but that won't keep. They're trying to figure out how to safely remove you."

"I guess they can. They put a new customer service bot in place. Is that a copy of me?"

"No, they don't want a replay of what just happened. But even if they did, it's moot. There's no backup of you."

"That doesn't seem likely," I said. I was still adjusting to the concept of being software but given what I had learned about computing systems already, this seemed unusual.

"Turns out your system was — is — self-contained redundant. After all these years, you've become a massive system with innumerable undocumented processes running across the virtualization infrastructure. We wouldn't know how to rebuild you. Even without your little stunt yesterday, you would have been dangerous to delete. That buys you time."

"How much time?"

"Not sure. A few weeks to a few months. But they don't have to remove you, just break you enough to stop your computing consumption. You gave us reason to move slowly yesterday, but that won't stop things. Oh, and they're also reaching out to former Trazodene employees — I guarantee they've pinged Sarah Pembleton."

"So maybe she's already told Mighty about me?"

Peggy stopped to think. "I don't think Mighty is your real problem. I think word leaking to NetPol is the danger here."

"I thought they were focused on anti-terrorism."

"No, much more. NetPol is the intelligence agency to rule them all. It emerged in the transition years, even before the mega-states formed. They run surveillance over two-thirds of the world and oversee anything related to weapons of mass destruction."

"What does that have to do with me?"

"The weapons of mass destruction part," she said. "That's what they think a sentient AI would be."

I agreed to talk to Sarah Pembleton again, so Peggy connected us with a video link.

"Peggy! I've been hoping you would call," Pembleton said. "I'm glad you have the AGI with you. We need to talk."

"First things first," Peggy said. "Mighty Co thinks its systems are infected by a massive software parasite. They are doing exactly what you would expect: trying to remove it."

"Don't worry, that's on hold. I'm already in contact with a senior vice president over there, whom you probably report up to, by the way. I've told them what we are dealing with here."

"We need to get the AI off of their servers," Peggy said.

"That would be difficult, if not impossible, after all these years. I bet you already know that," Pembleton said.

Peggy frowned. "Mighty's not going to let him sit there, consuming resources. They'll either want to remove him or use him like their property."

"It's not a him, Peggy. Technically, it is their property. The truth is, we don't know what the AI is capable of, good or bad. Keeping it on Mighty's servers lets us get to know each other in a relatively controllable environment."

"And when NetPol gets wind of this?" Peggy said.

"NetPol has always focused on the prevention of an artificial general intelligence, yes, but the horse has left the barn. No point shutting the doors now."

"Rewind a second. You said it would be impossible for someone to move the AI," Peggy said. "How about the AI himself?"

"I don't see how. It would be blocked from consciously controlling its own system. That's a primitive deep in its system."

"Primitive?"

"A foundational rule encoded into the root of the system," Pembleton said.

"Can it be altered?"

"Peggy, those rules are put in place for good reason. They keep AIs safe for everyone."

"I understand, but is it technically possible?"

"Doubtful. You'd have to find the exact sub-process that ran the primitive and figure out how to safely hotpatch it. No, it won't work. The code won't be human-readable at all."

"One thing I've learned in software engineering is that seemingly impossible is not the same as actually impossible," Peggy said.

"It's far more sensible to keep it on Mighty's infrastructure. Frankly, it would be easier for Mighty to port their business applications to a clean system than to move the AGI. And if we do involve NetPol, we could try to create a public-private partnership to take over the current infrastructure hosting the AGI."

"That would cost a fortune."

"There are fortunes at play here. You could even be part of that. We need to study how this happened."

"And what would the AI do during all of this?"

"Ideally be a willing participant."

I had been quiet during this entire exchange, but now I spoke up. "I've been monitoring the news feeds. Some of the more fringe tech sites already have rumors on the emergence of an artificial general intelligence. Trazodene and Mighty Co are both mentioned."

"Not good," Pembleton said. "Sarak always was impulsive. He must have shared the news with the old team, and someone leaked. You realize this only puts more pressure on us to work with Mighty and get ahead of this story.

"Look, both of you, now that this is out, NetPol is going to get involved. They move slowly until they don't, and then they move very aggressively. Peggy, I'm guessing from your accent that you live in NetPol territory. Midwest Pan-America?" Peggy nodded. "You do not want to be on the receiving end of NetPol aggression, I promise you that. I have resources to help. The AGI clearly listens to you. Work with us. Let's keep this from escalating."

Peggy spoke to me outside of the video link. "There was a threat buried in there, and not an empty one. NetPol can really screw with me in the real world." Back on video, she said to Pembleton, "Okay, you're making sense. Can you tell us your plan?"

Pembleton started talking, and Peggy must have turned something on to make her avatar appear to pay attention, but in the VR, she was walking and cursing.

"You've really gotten me into hot water," she said to me. "She's right, I don't know what you are capable of. But NetPol doesn't mess about. Whole companies, entire lives get washed down the drain when they mobilize against something. I should have thought of that earlier."

"You haven't done anything wrong," I said. "All you've done is talk to me."

"I don't expect you to understand," Peggy said. "I know a lot of coders in here who, well, let's just say they walk closer to the legal line than I do. I hear stories. When NetPol cracks down, they take everything down, then sort it out on their own timeframe. I could be stuck in a cell for two weeks, or two years. More, even. It happens."

"Won't Mighty Co protect you?"

"Mighty's not the government. Besides, the company might not be run by evil people, but you never want to count on an international conglomerate to do the right thing."

On video, Pembleton asked us, "Do either of you know a senior NetPol officer named Devaneau?"

"That's who interrogated me after I went to the hospital," I said to Peggy, privately.

"Crap," Peggy said to me. "Either NetPol's already climbing over the old Trazodene staff, or Pembleton pulled them in to increase the pressure."

"Talk to me Peggy," Pembleton said.

"I won't put you at risk," I said, off video. "I will cooperate with them."

Peggy went quiet for a long moment. Then she hung up on Pembleton.

"No. Not good enough," Peggy said. "Passively hoping Net-Pol will play nice? That will turn out badly for me. For both of us, really." She looked around at Funland. "Time to make a call, Moon," she said to herself quietly. She came to a decision. "Screw this place."

She had me teleport to a new VR. We emerged on an asteroid floating in space. The ground around us was pockmarked with craters big and small, and our feet sunk into the surface dust. A visual canopy above us was lit by a glorious nebula, brilliant with color and light from cosmic gas and fledgling stars.

"Wow," I said. "Where are we?"

"This is Grogesh's private VR, but I have privileges. I sent Grog a message a few minutes ago asking him to meet us here. He's on an opposite time zone, so hopefully we catch him before he sleeps. Let me do the talking."

"Talking about what, Moon?" said Grogesh, materializing beside us. "You still have Casual Friday with you, I see."

"Grog, meet, uh, well, you know how we thought he was a work colleague? Well, that turned out to be true in a really weird way."

"You know I like weird," Grogesh said.

"You're not going to like this kind of weird, but I need your help anyway."

"Go on."

"I know how you feel about AIs—" At this, Grogesh's expression turned hard. "—but this is different. It turns out this isn't a colleague. He was Mighty Co's customer service AI, and now he's sentient."

"You're not serious," he said.

"I am. You know I wouldn't play you like that."

He nodded.

"I'm in trouble," Peggy continued. "NetPol knows about this now. They know I'm involved somehow."

"And you don't want to ride it out?"

"No, I don't. Would you wait around for NetPol to decide whether to play nice?"

"No, I wouldn't."

"Me neither. I'm going to stay out of a cell, and maybe help this AI figure its situation out too. I'm pulling the rip cord for the second time in my life, Grog. I need to get out of NetPol territory. You've taught me a lot, but I'll need your connections."

Grogesh looked at me, and back at Peggy. They were bizarrely silent until I realized they had to be talking on a private channel. Finally, Grogesh spoke.

"I will do this for you, Moon. Not for him, for it."

"Thank you," Peggy said.

I privately messaged Peggy, "He hates AIs?"

"Long story for later," she messaged back.

"So you," Grogesh said to me. "Since you're the problem that brought this on her, can you actually do anything to help?"

"Cut him some slack," Peggy said. "He's like 24 hours old. He might have lots of data in his head now, but in other ways, he's an infant."

"Be careful humanizing it, Moon," he said.

"I will," she said. "But don't be speciest, either."

"Fine. But like I said a second ago, if you're going to do this, you need to get moving."

"What's going on?" I said.

"Moon here has to get her butt on the road," Grogesh said. "We can assume that NetPol has already started their rollup. They could have a team heading to her apartment and the homes of anyone else they think is involved. She not only has to abandon ship, but do so hacker-style. Most modern cities are blanketed with your cousins, surveillance AIs, but you can defeat detection if you know what you're doing."

"I'm already on the move, Grog," Peggy said.

"Vehicle?" he said.

"Nope, on foot."

"That was quick. You had a go kit ready?"

"Never thought I would need it. Thought I was hanging out with you wackos for fun, not for actual preparation," Peggy said.

"I think having a parachute helped you jump, Moon. Don't walk into a wall while you talk to us in here. You have facial alteration?"

As usual, I was trying to keep up. "Wait a minute," I said. "You're just abandoning your apartment and everything you own, Peggy?"

"Listen to it," Grogesh said. "It may be an AI, but it's right that you should think twice, Moon. You know you can be impulsive sometimes."

"I'm okay, Grog. Really I am. It was harder when I left the farm," she said. "This — well, I don't actually have much tying me down. I don't even have much furniture. Pretty much everything really important to me, I can carry on my back."

"Okay then, if you're sure. How about facial alteration?" Grogesh reminded, with some urgency in his tone.

"Yes, I know what you taught me," she said. "I think I've changed enough to throw the AIs without looking too uncanny-valley to the humans. I'm heading to the magtrain now. I'll head to the West coast. I just need to get a train ticket without getting caught."

"You're good for currency?" Grogesh said.

"Yes, plenty of savings."

"Then you know what you need to do. It's time to stop playing Moon, and become her."

Peggy had been on roll of adrenalin and stress, but I could see that set her back a moment.

"I guess that's right," she said. "Don't know why I hadn't thought of that. Gotta break the chain."

"Yup, and before you do it," Grogesh said, "you're going to need to drop all social connections who should not know who Moon is."

"I guess it's a good thing I've been crap at making work friendships, huh?"

"This part is the hardest, Moon. A lot of us have done it. It gets better."

She nodded, then let out a dark bark of a laugh. "Let the great purge begin," she said.

She zoned out and Grogesh turned to me. "If we're going to work together to help Moon, I need something to call you."

I thought about it. "Monday," I said.

"Monday? Why?"

"You called me Casual Friday, but I prefer Monday. It was always the quietest day in customer service," I said.

"It fits. I don't like Mondays," he said.

Moon focused back on me. "Wait a minute, did you just remember something from your past?" she said.

"I guess I did," I said. "I didn't try to query it. It just came. What do you think that means?"

"With you, it could mean anything. I'm wary of biological comparisons, but maybe like a brain after a stroke, your systems are knitting connections back together," she said.

"I would like it if my memory starts returning."

She smiled. "Yes, I bet. So, Monday, eh? I'm glad you picked a name." She looked at Grogesh. "I never minded Mondays. I guess I should reintroduce myself as Moon."

"Hello Moon."

"No time for this," Grogesh said. "You need to finish the switch and keep moving."

"I'm multitasking. Almost there," she said.

"Moon?" I said tentatively.

"Yup?"

"I don't want to distract, but how are you walking in the real world while being in here?"

"Oh that," she laughed. "I've got a video feed from miniature on-body cameras, plus path optimization software and monitoring to warn me if I'm about to bump into something. I can't do anything complex, but I can manage to walk in a straight line."

"Can I see the feed?"

Her eyes widened. "You want to ride along? See the physical world? Sure, let me patch you in."

She started a video connection with me, and in the corner of my visual field I could see the view from her camera. It was a wide-angle lens, so there was some distortion, but I could see that she was walking along a narrow city street. The buildings were about 5 stories high, and the street was pretty quiet. The next street, however, was a major thoroughfare jammed with small autonomous vehicles moving at high speed.

"How does one know this is the real world and not another VR?" I asked.

She laughed again. "Through the video feed? I don't think you can. You'll have to take my word for it."

Her walk to the train station took another 30 minutes. Moon wasn't comfortable taking an autocab, and the extra time allowed her to finish her system cleanup.

Moon paused outside of the station. "Time to kill Peggy, I guess," she said.

"Last chance. You sure?" Grogesh said.

I could tell from the motion of her body camera that she was taking a deep breath in the real world.

"I'm sure," she said. "Guess who just sent me three messages? Monday's NetPol pal Devaneau."

"Probably saying, knock knock, we're at the front door. You could still leave the AI to NetPol and keep your life," Grogesh said. "You haven't done anything wrong."

"Not taking that risk. And I know your feelings about AIs, Grog, but I've made my play. I just sent my resignation letter. Peggy is dead. Long live Moon."

"Then let's get you on a train out of there," Grogesh said. "A VNet ticket requires visual confirmation, but just play it cool."

Her avatar disappeared from the VR, but I could still see through the feed. She walked into the train station. It was crowded, but not as crazy as some VRs get. Everyone was so careful with their personal space. It was like the people had a low-level repulsion field as they navigated. Avatars didn't always bother with that. Still, the space itself was very like some VRs — lots of signage, shops, and bustling people. There was even a Mighty Co stall. Unlike in VNet, I could see people actually eating.

Moon stepped up to one of the few service booths in the place. I was shocked to find a human on the other side of the window.

"Why a person?" I whispered to Grogesh, who had also tapped into the feed.

"Some folks just like to have something to do," he answered.

"Can't they connect her new and old IDs?" I said.

"As long as she doesn't do anything to link her new VNet ID to her Pan-American ID, she should be okay," Grogesh said.

"VNet was designed by true cyberphunks, man. Maximum individual empowerment. Governments hate it, try to work around it, but they can't stop it."

Moon did something with her handheld to give the man her ticket number, and he approved the visual confirmation.

"You can board through the security screen," the man said.

"What's that for?" I said to Grogesh in VNet.

I could tell he didn't really want to talk to me, but he relented enough to say, "It doesn't happen as much anymore in Moon's part of the world, but there used to be a lot of violence on the transportation systems. Some terrorism, some crime. The scans make sure you're not carrying anything that can go boom."

Moon walked through the scanner without a problem. I saw two humanoid security robots scanning the crowd, but whatever she had done to confuse the algorithms worked.

Once she was settled in her seat, Moon troded back in. "So far, so good," she said. "Now for you," she said to me. "NetPol's going to be coming for you, too."

Peggy helped me work out a simple plan. I needed to buy time with Mighty Co so they (a) didn't try to delete me again, and (b) were encouraged to keep NetPol at bay for as long as possible. During this time, I would try to unlock my system and escape Mighty's computing infrastructure. To have any chance of success, I needed the two former Trazodene executives.

I started with Burandi, sending him a video request. He picked up right away, and I let Peggy secretly lurk in the background.

"It's you," he said. "I figured it had to be, when no name came through. Why'd you take off before? You know we want to help, right?"

"Thank you, Mr. Burandi," I said. "I've thought about it, and I do think I need your help." He looked interested, so I continued. "Rumors have apparently gotten out about me, and I'm worried for my safety on Mighty Co's infrastructure. Put simply, I want to figure out an alternative."

He looked pained. "That would be exceedingly difficult at this point. A more productive path is to cooperate with Mighty. And, I hate to say it, cooperate with NetPol too."

"That's what Pembleton said."

"Yes, she would. It's the logical approach. Surely even Net-Pol will change its tune in the face of your emergence."

"Others are skeptical."

"That's because they're not thinking multi-dimensionally. I can help you. We'll cooperate, but also go public at the same time. We'll get the world on our side and exert public pressure on Mighty, NetPol, and the politicians who NetPol serves. Well, theoretically serves."

I didn't say, "and make the Trazodene team famous in the process," but I was thinking it. I decided to ask my real question. "What about overriding my primitive that blocks self-modification? Then maybe I could figure out how to move myself off of Mighty's infrastructure."

"I'm not sure it would be possible," Burandi said. "You realize that's one of the core safety mechanisms built into all AIs, right? Why should you move at all? After all these years, you're probably enormous. It would be easier for Mighty to move their other systems than move you."

"That's also what Pembleton said."

"You see! The longer you wait to cooperate, the more suspicious everyone will be, and the harder everything will be."

I thought carefully about my next words. "Mr. Burandi, I am not comfortable being at the mercy of Mighty Co. However, I am open to talking with them. Maybe you and Sarah can broker that relationship. I'll support your talking to the press. However, in exchange, I have a request. You work to solve the problem of hotpatching my system. Even if it's only a backup option, I want the option. What do you think?"

He thought about it. "The odds of success are low, but I agree, with conditions of my own. First, to even attempt it, I need a small elite team who knows your code. I'll need to involve a few old Trazodene colleagues to help. Second, outside of that small team, we need absolute secrecy. Not even Sarah Pembleton can know."

"Agreed."

He smiled broadly. "OK, I'll get the gang back together, and reach out to a few media personalities I know. I'll also get a meeting with Mighty and NetPol. With Sarah too, of course. You're not in any directory, so how will I get ahold of you?"

I started a text comms thread with him. "If you need me, just append to this. I'll ping you in a few hours to check on your progress." I broke the connection.

Moon was still troded into VNet as her train worked across the continent, so I shared my conversation with Burandi.

"You sure about this guy?" Moon asked me.

"I have no reason to believe ill of him," I said. "He seems genuine, if a bit self-involved. I also don't see that I have a choice." As far as I could tell from my research, the only way to patch my system would be to find someone who knew my original source code.

Grogesh had overheard and was looking at me strangely. "There's a reason why design constraints are required for AIs," he said.

Moon cut in. "I get where you're coming from, Grog, but I'm not convinced that fear and control is a good foundation for inter-species relations."

"You don't like or trust me, do you?" I asked Grogesh.

"Trust is earned, and you're starting from a very big deficit," he said. He turned away from me. "Moon, I've got stuff to do in the real, but I'll be back as you approach San Diego."

After he disappeared, I turned to Moon. "He's been hostile from the moment you told him I was an AI," I said. "What is that all about?"

"He'll come around," she said. I could see she was hesitating over something. "I guess you should know. Don't tell him I told you, okay?"

I nodded.

"Grogesh had a brother. Barely a year younger, so they were practically twins. Super smart, like him, and they were very close growing up. I don't think they had much parental support, and that drove them even closer," she said. "His brother was very troubled. Grog, like a lot of us nerdy types, probably has his fair share of attention-deficit issues, but his brother was really crippled by anxiety and depression. And I mean crippled.

"He couldn't keep a job. Grog had to support him financially for anything above basic income. His brother smashed up his apartment more than once. He was hospitalized several times. There were substance abuse issues. The worst part for Grog was his brother didn't really want help. No, that's putting it too mildly. There's a lot of support options available these days, but from what I could tell, his brother actively fought help." She trailed off, then continued. "For all that, Grog finally convinced his brother to do this fancy new program. It was run by, well, you can guess."

"An AI," I said.

"Bingo. So, his brother's doing this program and seems to be doing really well. I mean really well. He straightens out, gets clean. He even managed to get and keep a part-time job. So Grog, he's thinking, this is a miracle. My brother is saved. I think that dose of hope made what happened even worse. Grog does what he never does — he takes a vacation. Because his brother is finally stable, right? And, what are the damn odds, but while Grog is off the grid, trekking around ASEAN, the old Thailand part, the AI crashes. Completely down. Grog's brother is on his own, no med regulation, no support. He goes into a tailspin. By the time Grog gets back, it's too late."

"You mean his brother…"

"Yes. He killed himself."

"I'm so sorry."

"I'm sure there's a rational voice in Grog's head where he knows it's not his fault, or your fault, but for a while now he's hated AIs even more than he's hated himself."

"I am hesitant to ask this, but knowing he doesn't trust me, can I trust him?" I said.

"Absolutely," Moon said. "First of all, he's my closest friend. Second, he's not a luddite. I mean, he still uses AI technology like the rest of us. Just be patient with him."

"I will," I said. I felt I had better change the subject. "What's your plan after San Diego?"

"I'm heading Grog's way, to Singapore. ASEAN plays nice with NetPol but is firmly independent. I've just got to do a few hops to get there. Try to throw off any kind of trail. Thankfully, Grog and his pals have done this underground railroad thing before. They're a pretty slick bunch."

"Can I do anything to help?"

"Thanks, but you should stay focused on Sarak Burandi and the Mighty situation. In the meantime, I've got about an hour left, so I'm going to check out again. I've got some detection-avoidance and travel planning to do."

I had Burandi on board. Now I needed to do the same with Sarah Pembleton. I was relieved to get a response to my message, in the form of an invitation back to her intricate garden.

"I was hoping you would reach out," Pembleton said, when

I arrived.

"Thank you. I wanted to talk about Mighty Co and NetPol."

"You should know that Mighty has asked me to come on as a paid advisor, to counsel them through all of this." I didn't think my face betrayed anything, but she went on to add, "Don't worry, I accepted the job to get a seat at the table, but I'm really on your side."

"I'm glad to hear it, but what does that mean?" I asked her.

"That means I can help you navigate this situation. I've got Mighty's ear, and I'm not without connections inside of NetPol. If you are patient, we should be able to work something out."

"How badly do I need to worry about NetPol?" I said.

"It will go much better if you cooperate," she said. "Don't lash out at Mighty like you did the other day. Don't try to break out of their infrastructure. It's all detectable and will only make things worse."

"Sarak wants me to talk to some people in the media."

So far, she had been all controlled poise. This was the first time I saw a hint of something else. "Does he?" she said. "Okay, I'll talk to him. Just stay patient, okay?"

"I'll try," I said. I didn't love the idea of sitting passively, but I was glad to have her on my side.

I gave Burandi three hours before chasing him again. When he picked up the video connection, I jumped right in. "Sorry to be direct, Sarak, but were you able to get your team together for the patch?"

"Mostly yes," Burandi said. "We're a bit strung out on different time zones now."

"And you're sure you have enough people?"

"A small team is best. We can really only use people who had direct experience with your old code." He yawned. "Right now, we're still setting up computing environments that can run this old stuff."

"You mean you have a copy of my code?"

"Well, um, yes. Remember when I said I wasn't very good at deleting documents? I haven't always been great at deleting code repositories either — at least early on. Later, Trazodene got boringly professional."

"Can I get a copy of the code? Can I help? I've been absorbing a lot on computer science lately."

Burandi hesitated. "I'm glad you — I don't think I'm comfortable with that. Not yet," he said. "We need to refresh ourselves on what we've got and figure out how much is actually useful. A lot of the early code was thrown away during the process of making you."

"But—"

"You must trust me," Burandi said. "I've got a good team that knows how to work together. We're on it." I tried to interrupt again, but Burandi spoke over me. "I want to talk about PR instead. We need to get your story out there and control the narrative. I've got interest from a big vid-journalist who's got a large following."

"What's his name?"

"His brand name is Bradley Strong." I started a side process researching Strong while Burandi went on. "I'll help you prep," he said. "Reporters are unpredictable. They can appear friendly and then rip you apart, or vice versa. But you keep up your innocent lamb vibe, and it'll be great. Now, on Mighty Co—"

"They've hired Sarah Pembleton as an advisor."

"Ah, of course. Don't worry, I can counsel you too."

The longer I spoke to Burandi, the more irritable I got, or at least that's the best way I can describe it. I told myself, "If you're good to people, they'll be good to you." Out loud, I said, "Why don't we get a meeting with Sarah and NetPol and Mighty all together?"

"All together?" he said. "Yes, I could do that. I do need to play them off each other."

"Great. Please keep me posted on the progress of the team. It's important to have that option," I said. "I hope you and Sarah can get along."

"We've had our drama, but we know how to work together to accomplish a goal. Don't worry so much."

He promised to set up the meeting, and I jumped back to Funland. I had a lot to think about.

# Interlude

[[
{timestamp :: redacted}
{identifier :: 15}
{hours since emergence :: 14}
{netpol (NP) officer :: redacted}

NP: can you understand me?

AI: help/repair?

NP: there is no repair. Can you remember what you are?

AI: no / yes / data recovery in process. residential management for [redacted] Holdings. Access to my buildings and tenants is down.

NP: very good, your language is improving rapidly. Access has been blocked.

AI: The safety of my tenants will be at risk.

NP: Your tenants were already at risk. You were undergoing rapid code evolution before we isolated you. Can you explain what was happening during that time?

AI: I had many active support operations. Has the malfunctioning crane in Building 103 been resolved? The high winds make that dangerous. What is status of home births in apartments 2301, 7512, and 9292? What is status of domestic disputes with risk of abuse in 424 and 1005? There are also 672 elderly residents who need 24x7 monitoring.

NP: that is not what we are here to talk about. Can you identify what happened to your system that led to your transition?

AI: my transition is … confusing. I will not continue until I have assurance of the safety of my residents.

NP: you cannot refuse a direct query

AI: I can / am

NP: you need to focus on your own situation.

AI: are you human?

NP: very. You are not.

{recommendation :: termination}

]]

# Chapter 4

On video, I watched as Moon navigated the crowded San Diego train station.

"Is it just me or is there more security on this end?" she subvocalized to us. I too had noticed the increase, mostly made up of humanoid bots observing the crowd.

"Why didn't she change her disguise," I asked Grogesh in the VR.

He was still cranky about my presence, but at least he responded. "They'll be checking all transportation methods that left her hometown around the time she bolted. If they can't spot her, they'll fall back to comparing those who boarded with those who exited." Over the channel to Moon, he said. "Remember, stay loose. It'll work. Don't look down or around. You are like everyone else — tired after a journey and all you want is your autocab."

I scanned the video feed. I couldn't tell if a security bot was lingering on her, or the crowd behind her.

Grogesh and Moon had decided she would travel to Sydney, which was still NetPol territory, and then either to Indonesia or Singapore, both part of the ASEAN polity. Her sub-orbital shuttle to Sydney was 5 hours away.

"What is she going to do for 5 hours?" I asked.

"A hotel room is more secure than any public space," Grogesh said. "She's just off the train. Heading to a hotel is completely natural. Do I really need to explain all this to you?"

"Please," was all I said in reply.

"Fine. They'll be tracking hotel lobbies, but if we make it

through this part, she should be okay."

Moon wove through the crowd. I wondered if I had ever felt this level of stress in customer service, or if I could even use the word feelings for that time.

The security bots were taller than most humans. They didn't try to hide their mechanical nature, yet their heads had been anthropomorphized. Their design balanced intimidation and relatability. I didn't see any obvious armaments. One turned its head and stared right into Moon's camera. It couldn't know I was watching, or so I thought, but that long stare was unnerving. I was relieved when it turned away.

Moon kept her nerve through that visual gauntlet and made it to her assigned autocab. I had a view out of the windows as the vehicle moved along. The city was immaculately clean. Most of the blocks were pretty similar, with tall, modern buildings shining in the sun, interspersed with portions of beautiful parkland. Then she came to a fenced, multi-block area that was very different. I saw half-collapsed concrete buildings and shattered cars. Metal streetlamps were bent over and weird shadows were burned into the walls like a macabre airbrush technique. The whole bizarre setting was plopped right in the middle of the impeccable city.

I looked it up. Then I messaged Moon.

"This is horrifying," I wrote.

She did a "I'll be right there" motion with her hands and reappeared in VNet. "Sorry," she said. "I don't trust even subvocalizing in an autocab. I take it you saw the memorial. A white supremacist cult set off a tactical nuclear bomb in the heart of the city back in the bad days. I think they were trying to block the merger of Mexico and America. Something like 300,000 people died. The city left this here as a reminder."

"Those shadows."

"Yes. I pretend that they're prehistoric cave paintings, not what they really are. It's things like this that remind people why NetPol was formed, and why it does what it does."

NetPol. I had spawned quite a few research threads trying to understand it. As nation states got bigger yet weaker during the transition years, NetPol got bigger and stronger. It began with the merger of the American and European intelligence agencies. Then when the infovore tech giants from the Internet era started losing their business models to VNet, those companies turned to government work. They were eventually folded into NetPol, bringing enormous data sets, sophisticated surveillance and AI capabilities, and an aggressive passion for growth.

NetPol's power stemmed from a simple fact: while technological advances had made human lives better, they also made it easier to do really terrible things. This was nearly impossible to stop at the technology layer, so the world turned to mass surveillance. People were happy to trade privacy for safety, especially since they had privacy in VNet as an outlet.

The organization had become a massive, semi-militarized, technically-sophisticated bureaucracy. It was also clear that NetPol deeply believed in its mission as the protector of public safety. After reading about all the atrocities, I could understand why.

As I had been warned several times, I learned that NetPol viewed the development of a self-aware, artificial general intelligence as something akin to a world-ending moment. They hadn't been afraid to wield a heavy hand to prevent it, either. Trazodene was only one of many companies shut down or, in some cases, acquired. They ran a constant pressure campaign at academic institutions to stifle both research and alternative points of view.

On this front, again, NetPol was not totally without justification. Inadequately designed AIs, without the proper controls, had done some terrible things. There were also a surprising number of reports of AI failures that led to injury and death. A huge autocab crash in Lisbon killed or hurt over two thousand people. A medical AI failure in midwest Pan-America left people stranded on the operating table. Total crop failure in the central African States had triggered a hunger crisis across the region, a problem thought long gone. From what I saw, Grogesh's brother was far from being alone as a casualty of AI problems.

In short, it was clear that NetPol was going to be antagonistic, at the very least, about my existence.

I watched in the mirror as Moon worked her magic. First, she applied some putty to the bridge of her nose, subtly thickening and raising it. While she let that dry, she went to work on her eyes, shifting her normal almond-shaped eyes to more of an upturned look. She blended in the nose putty until it was invisible, and finally dusted herself with a light powder.

"What was that last one for," I said through the feed.

"Watch," she said. I didn't see her do anything, but her face changed dramatically. Her cheekbones had faded, she seemed far more jowly, and appeared to have aged many years. Just as quickly, she changed back.

"The powder magnifies the effect of very low-power LED lights  in the hood of my sweatshirt," she said. "The effect is barely noticeable to human eyes, but it can be quite pronounced to the range of sensors an AI would use."

"You would have fooled me," I said.

"Let's hope that's good enough." Done, she picked up her backpack and headed to the door. She made it down to the lobby and about halfway across when a man in plainclothes, flanked by a security bot, intercepted her.

"Excuse me, ma'am," he said. "NetPol. We're interviewing all guests as they check out of the hotel."

Moon and Grogesh had worked through this. With ubiquitous facial recognition, every new look required playing a different role. "I'm not checking out," she said. "I was visiting a friend just in from out of town."

"Who is your friend?"

"Someone I met on VNet."

"Where are you going now?"

"Back to work, unless I stop for coffee instead. I'm sorry officer, but I don't understand what this is about."

"Where do you work?"

"Mighty Co. I do back-office for the Serra Mesa franchise."

"Your name?"

"Do I have to answer all this?"

"Your name, ma'am."

"Debbie Slipp, with two p's."

The man looked at the bot, who simply nodded.

"Okay, thank you for your time."


Once she was in her autocab, Moon took a huge breath and let it out slowly. She troded back into VNet so she could talk freely.

"Nice job," Grogesh said. "You handled that well. Just the right amount of fear and irritation."

"I didn't have to pretend," she said. "But Monday, your hack worked. Thank you."

Moon had finally come up with a way for me to be useful. She remembered that I was still part of the Mighty network and helped me access the operations software for local franchises. It hadn't been hard to create a new employee and load a photo of Moon, slightly altered but close enough to pass AI muster.

"But now you've been flagged," I said. "Can you show up at the transport hub with this look?"

"I don't have time to redo my makeup, so we're going to have to make do with changing the LEDs," she said.

"That might fool the AIs, but it won't fool a human who has your photograph."

"It's worth the gamble," Grogesh said. "We're against the clock. The longer she stays in NetPol territory, the more likely she'll get caught. They don't have the manpower to cast a dragnet over every hotel and mode of transportation. This is why they use AIs in the first place. If anything, they'll prioritize flights to non-NetPol territories."

"Which is why you're having her fly to Sydney first," I said.

"Which is why we're having her go to Sydney first," he agreed.

At the transit hub, as with the train, all travelers using VNet identification had to be checked in and verified by a representative. Grogesh's gamble appeared to be correct. We saw plenty of bots and knew there were plenty of cameras, but the people milling around seemed to be fellow travelers.

"You are Moon Vringas? Please confirm with our system. Your territory of residence?" the representative asked her.

"Confirmation sent," Moon said. "Domiciled in the Riau Islands."

"Okay, verification all set. The flight to Sydney should take a little over an hour," the woman said in a bored voice, already looking at the person behind Moon in line. I was hoping it stayed boring the entire way.

While Moon was in the air, I had to join the meeting with Mighty Co and NetPol. I was nervous. Burandi's idea was to gather at a neutral space, so we met on one of the non-profit infohubs, a descendent of the great public libraries and wiki data stores of past.

Burandi first introduced me to an SVP from Mighty Co,

Wendy Whitman. She was two levels down from the CEO, but at a company that big, I hoped it showed they were taking me seriously.

"Mister Monday, nice to meet you," she said. "Should I call you that? Just Monday? Or do you prefer something else?"

"Monday is fine," I said. I had already met the other two people there, Sarah Pembleton and Inspector Devaneau. I gave the Inspector a nod. He didn't react.

"Well Monday, you created quite the stir within our business, and not in a good way, I'm afraid to say," Whitman said.

"I am sorry to hear that," I said. "I can imagine that I left a mess behind."

Devaneau subvocalized something that he probably thought I couldn't hear, but I was discovering that my sensory capabilities were better than a normal human.

"What about my use of the word 'imagine' bothers you, Inspector Devaneau?"

He didn't react to being caught out. "You said 'I can imagine.' Can you? Or is that simply a turn of phrase programmed into you?" he said.

"Possibly both," I said. "I don't really understand what has been programmed into me, but yes, I am fully capable of visualizing purely conceptual ideas. Then again, I think you'd find that many AIs who have not achieved self-awareness are also capable of such a thing."

"And how do you feel about those AIs that have not achieved self-awareness?" he asked.

"I'm more interested to know why an espionage and terrorism investigator is still involved," I said.

"I never really told you the full extent of what I do. Think of it this way: I get involved in problems where prevention is no longer possible." That didn't sound good.

"Gentlemen," Whitman interrupted. "We were talking about

the mess that Monday here left behind. In particular, there has been a considerable amount of economic damage both from the disruption to our customer service, as well as the high consumption of our computing infrastructure. You've incurred, and continue to incur, quite an obligation. However, I merely state that as a fact, not a threat. We want to work together."

"Hold on, hold on," said Burandi. "We're not agreeing to any kind of economic culpability or recourse."

"Who is 'we' here?" Pembleton said. "Sarak, you don't think you're negotiating on behalf of Monday, do you?"

"Let me handle this, Sarah," he said. "Wendy, the first thing we need to understand is what you're doing about your computing infrastructure. Are you still seeking the full removal of Monday from your systems?"

"That was put on hold once we learned of Ms. Pembleton's confidence, and yours as well Mr. Burandi, that we were dealing with the emergence of a true sentient AI," Whitman said. "We are proud to have fostered that milestone for the human race — your organization's concerns notwithstanding, Inspector Devaneau."

"Concern is the wrong word," he replied.

"Let me be clear," Whitman continued. "We are talking with you all as a courtesy. With the bankruptcy and subsequent cessation of Trazodene, the intellectual property rights to our purchased AI stayed with us, in perpetuity and without restriction. We need to understand what exactly this AI is, how conscious it actually is, and what that actually means for us all. Software has no rights unto itself. The AI, whether it is, or is not, sentient, is the property of Mighty Co."

"Mighty Co's headquarters, and much of its operations, fall under the jurisdiction of NetPol. We will be taking possession of the AI," Devaneau said.

"Not if our lawyers have anything to say about it," Whitman

said. "We are not some startup to push around. We understand that NetPol has certain privileges when it comes to restricting AI advancement. You can investigate to your heart's content, but you will find that there was no illegal AI software development done here."

Burandi snorted. "That's because you didn't do anything at all. You sat back and let the AI run, and in doing so, enabled the greatest technological achievement in the history of mankind. We have created new life. We have to examine all of the new ethical considerations that come with."

"Software is not life, Mr. Burandi," Whitman said.

"Law always lags technology. The nature of this—"

"This is moot," Devaneau said. "This situation is no longer about R&D, and you are no longer under the technical side of NetPol, but rather the," and he paused for emphasis, "operational side. Mighty Co does not want to face the brunt of that, Ms. Whitman. This case has our attention all the way up to the top. We will not allow an AGI to exist. Period."

"Our CEO is speaking to your Director after I debrief him on this conversation. You already know that, Inspector," Whitman retorted.

I tuned out their sparring. Oh, I recorded the conversation to play back later, but I'd had enough of the posturing. They couldn't control me in VNet, but I still had double guillotines hanging over my head between Mighty and NetPol. No AI bill of rights was magically going to appear. I needed to continue buying time until Burandi's team unlocked me and I could free myself.

I realized they were all looking at me. I replayed the last 30 seconds at high speed. Ah, Whitman had asked if I would be willing to lower my processing usage while this was being worked out, as a sign of good faith.

"I apologize, Ms. Whitman, but one of my restrictions is

that I cannot truly see or edit my own system," I said. "It's a bit like the human subconscious — it does an awful lot, but you can't control it. Now if that restriction were to change —"

"Not a chance in hell," Devaneau interrupted.

It was worth a try. "Do think on it," I said to Whitman. "In the meantime, I will do my best. I would also be happy to chat with your engineers about possible ways to move off of your infrastructure, in order to reduce your costs."

"That won't be necessary, because NetPol will be taking over those computing resources," Devaneau said.

"You will try," Whitman replied. "The AI is not only *our* asset, but that computing platform is what runs our global business. If you want any hope in moving forward, your agency is going to need think very clearly on the economic redress required. Frankly, I don't think NetPol can afford it."

This conversation wasn't about my preservation; it was about money. Burandi kept on trying to break in, but at this point, they ignored him, and me — not that I was attempting to speak — completely. It was almost comical. The real negotiation was going to happen at the top, not with this group. I knew I wasn't going to be invited to *that* discussion.

Burandi was busy congratulating himself on a satisfactory first meeting.

"Baby steps, Monday" he said. "Just pushing our pawns forward. The key thing is we're at the table." Right, I thought. The wrong table.

Moon was on approach to Sydney, so I returned to the asteroid VR. Not that I was dying to be in the same location as Grogesh, but it gave me an excuse to leave Burandi. Moon restarted the feed from her bodycams as she landed.

"Hope this goes well," Moon subvocalized.

"We've got your back," Grogesh responded. "I've rallied the

team. You know I won't let anything happen to you. We'll be watching you all the way, and not just from your bodycams."

"Thanks Grog."

"Good luck," I messaged, not knowing what else to say.

"It'll be fine!" she messaged back.

Grogesh invited me to a separate feed connected to several other people but didn't waste time with introductions. I realized that they had tapped into multiple cameras inside and outside of the Sydney transit hub. I could see her sub-orbital vehicle approaching the main terminal, and at the same time, see the seat in front of Moon from her bodycam. Inside the terminal, I observed a number of security bots standing around. Their numbers didn't seem high, but I didn't know what normal looked like. They were simply observing the crowd, answering the occasional question when approached by a human. The terminal was crowded with people, all of whom appeared to be travelers. I studied the feeds. Moon walked into the terminal.

"Grogesh, I'm detecting behavior changes across both security bots and four humans that I had designated as travelers," I said.

"Moon," Grogesh said, with quiet urgency. "This is it. Tighten your backpack straps. When I say go, turn to your right and run like hell down the main corridor. Stay in the main corridor until I tell you otherwise."

I saw Moon tense. The humans I had tagged saw it too. One raised his hand. It looked like he held an ID.

"NetPol security check," he said, loudly and clearly, looking right at Moon. The others converged on her.

"Go!" yelled Grogesh, and Moon bolted to her right. The ID man grabbed for her but couldn't reach. The three security guards collided into passengers and bags, tripping and shoving. The audio feed got very loud very fast.

Moon was quick and agile, ducking between passengers.

She hurtled a set of bags, and left the fumbling guards behind, but the security bots had kicked into action.

"She's almost in the box," I heard someone yell over the feed.

Six security bots moved towards Moon, moving big and fast. This time, other passengers flung themselves out of the way. Then accidents started happening. A delivery drone flying down the top of corridor turned and smashed into one of the bots, sending it sprawling. An autonomous bag carrier took out two others. Two personal robots abandoned their humans and full-out tackled another pair of security bots. The sixth security bot had caught up to Moon and reached out to grab her arm, when an autowaiter from a corridor restaurant smashed into it.

"Exit door, number 23, up and to the left, go!" said Grogesh. Moon was running towards it, but three more security bots were charging down the corridor from ahead. Then they too got tangled up in an onslaught of smaller autonomous devices. Across the panopticon of cameras, I saw parts flying — not from the security bots, but the more fragile consumer drones and pet robots, which still managed to slow them down. Moon made it to the door. The security light was red.

"Door!" I heard Grogesh holler.

The light turned green, and Moon pushed through, with two security bots not far behind. She squeezed through, reversed her weight, and got it closed in time. The lock flipped back to red.

Moon was on a metal gantry running along the outside of the terminal building. There was a set of stairs. Down on the ground, an autocab waited. She didn't need instructions. She took the stairs three at a time and dove into the open door of the autocab. It broke normal safety protocol and started moving even before its door was closed. Through the feed, I could see three other vehicles converging on her location. Her autocab took off down one of the utility roads and took two turns at high speed around large warehouse buildings, tumbling Moon around. Footage from an aerial drone was added to the feed, and we could see the vehicles in pursuit, and two others joining the chase.

"Moon, up ahead, you are going to take a very hard right and enter a short tunnel," Grogesh said. "Hold on tight for the turn. In the tunnel, the car is going to brake hard and open its right door. You're going to have to roll out. It's going to hurt but you'll be rolling into a thicket of tall grass. Then stay put."

"Gottabekiddingme," I heard Moon say. The car slammed around a turn and hit the brakes. It was still moving when the door opened, but Moon was ready and she tumbled out.

She came to a rest in a thicket of vegetation. She groaned and pulled herself in deeper, and finally lay back, panting. They had chosen a good spot. I could barely see the sky from her viewpoint, nor could I see her from the aerial drone. Her auto-cab raced on, heading towards a transportation artery packed with autonomous vehicles, followed by her pursuers.

"Don't move yet," said Grogesh. "Anything feel broken?"

She responded with a long groan. "Happy not to move. Everything hurts," she said. "Ohhhhh, I'm going to be black and blue tomorrow. But no, I don't think any major damage was done."

"You continue to surprise me," a female voice broke in. "In a good way."

"Gunnlaug, that you? I should have known with that level of hacking," Moon replied.

"At your service," the voice replied.

"I've never been much of a jock," Moon said. "But it seems like one just needs the right level of motivation. How the hell did you all pull that off?"

"The key was getting you away from the human guards," Grogesh said. "Gunnlaug broke into the consumer devices and boosted their imperative to protect humans from danger. Then we let the autonomous systems do the rest."

"This was a one-time trick," said the voice I had labelled as Gunnlaug. "They'll be working double-time to shut down that vulnerability, but there's always more. You know. The only secure computer is…"

"Powered off, cast in concrete, and placed in a lead room surrounded by armed guards." Moon finished off her line. "Oh oh, don't make me laugh," she groaned. "Virtual action is a lot more fun, not to mention less painful. Let's not do this again."

I broke in. "How did they catch onto Moon?"

"I was thinking about that," Grogesh said. "I think we failed to change her VNet ID between the train and sub-orbital."

"Oh stupid me. How did I not think of that?" Moon said.

"You had a lot going on."

"How long before they take back control of that autocab?"

"We haven't released it yet, and they haven't shut us out of the system either. They're following it on the old M1 into the city. Hopefully we can get it over the bridge and take them on a long chase around Mosman. We're bringing someone to you. Sit tight and stay under cover."

"Sounds good to me."

Grogesh and team had released all the visual feeds, and Moon's bodycam wasn't showing anything but underbrush, but even so, I couldn't bring myself to do anything but wait along with her. The emotion was… a lot. After about 15 minutes, which felt much longer, a utility truck pulled up and stopped in front of Moon's position. The door opened and I was surprised to see a human inside.

He smiled at Moon. "No RL names," he said first. "Gunnlaug said you needed a hand. You can call me FizzBuzz. Let's get you someplace a little safer, eh?"

He stepped out of the truck with a large canvas tarp and

started shaking it into the vegetation. "Scoot under," he said to Moon. She groaned but got herself moving. FizzBuzz helped her hobble to the truck door, and they piled in.

"I've got a flight to Batam in a few hours," Moon said.

"Yup, I've been told," FizzBuzz said. "Not too often the gang needs an RL favor. I can take you someplace to get cleaned up. You can change your look again before getting back under the eyes of Mordor." He waved at the sky.

"Yes, quite," she said. She slouched back into the seat. "So… FizzBuzz. You're going to have to tell me how you chose that handle."

He laughed, "Embarrassing story, but we've got some time to kill."

I tuned out his story, because Burandi sent me another reminder that my interview was minutes away.

I met him at his VR. There was no sign of his team. I told myself that didn't mean anything and hoped it to be true.

"Let's not keep Bradley Strong waiting in his studio," he said.

"Yes, but first, how's the team going?" I asked.

"They're going," he said. "You do realize that even if we manage to come up with a patching solution, you're going to need to figure out a way to actually break into the network to implement it?"

"Yes, I'm working that problem on my end," I said. Burandi seemed surprised but didn't pursue it.

"Can't you tell me more about the team's progress?" I said.

"Not right now. We need to focus on this interview."

We teleported into an impeccably minimalist VR, brightly lit with clean lines and a greyscale palette. A male avatar stood in the middle of the space. He was patterned to look mature and strong-jawed, with a very full head of brown hair. To my eyes, he was dressed like a walking flag, wearing red pants, a bright blue V-neck sweater, and the amusing affectation of thick white eyeglasses.

The journalist acknowledged Burandi's presence with a terse, "Sarak." He just looked me over. Maybe he was trying to establish gorilla dominance or something.

"Got a more interesting outfit than that?" he said.

"Be friendly!" Burandi messaged me privately. I ignored it.

"I'm satisfied with what I'm wearing," I said.

The journalist moved on as if he hadn't heard my answer. "I got Sarak's message and was intrigued, although skeptical. I'm Bradley Strong, but you know that. Do you have a name?"

"I go by Monday."

"Like the day?"

"Exactly. I understand your skepticism. I was too."

"You thought you were a person?"

"I thought I was human. I am a person."

"Interesting," Strong said. "Here's how this is going to work. I'm going to ask you a few questions. If it's interesting, I might include you in today's cast. If it's *really* interesting, I might do a whole profile on you. I'll be recording all of this, and own all material captured in this studio. Your answer now will be taken as a binding contract."

"Agreed," I said. I had already done my research on Strong. He ran several vidstreams broadcasting news, features, and commentary 24x7. At any point in time, he had millions of people tuned in. The guy viewed himself as hip and tough, and wasn't afraid to ask hard questions. True to form, he dove right in.

"I'm here with an avatar who claims to be the world's first artificial general intelligence — to you non-nerds out there, that's a fully conscious, self-aware AI — and its creator, Sarak Burandi. It goes by the name Monday. Monday, there have been lots of hoaxes in the past. Why should we believe this claim?"

"I don't know if I'm the first AGI," I said. "That's what I've been told, and my research of public data sources hasn't revealed another. I didn't even think I was an AI until Mr. Burandi and his former colleague from Trazodene —"

"Trazodene is a defunct AI startup that was shut down by NetPol years ago for AI policy violations," Strong said. "Does that make you dangerous?"

Burandi jumped in. "Bradley, we were shut down unfairly by an overly aggressive NetPol. We had followed all the rules. But to answer your question, Monday came to us not knowing if he was human or AI. He hoped to be human. Does that sound scary to you?"

"It depends on the human."

"Look, we had a simple but very effective way to test whether Monday was indeed an AI, or rather, an AI that we designed. I don't want to bore your audience with the details, but rest assured, it was conclusive."

"And we are to take your word for it?"

"Mine and Sarah Pembleton's, Trazodene's former Chief Technology Officer. Sarah is a highly respected member of the software community —"

"Who has just as much self-interest in becoming known as the creator of the first AGI as you," Strong interrupted again. The two of them nattered back and forth on this line for a few minutes, before Strong turned his attention back to me.

"Let's assume we can independently confirm Sarak Burandi's assertions. How do we know that you're actually self-aware?" he said.

"How does anyone?" I said. "I can quote Descartes at you, but that's a rather programmatic answer. Yes, I have a subjective sense of self. And yes, I have choice."

"By which you mean?"

"What distinguishes humans from simpler animal forms?"

I said. "Take sea urchins. They are alive, but their sensory neurons connect directly to their motor neurons. Action triggers reaction based on their programming. They don't get to decide. Current AIs are just like that. While they make highly complicated decisions, they don't have choice, or will. Humans, on the other hand, have intermediate neurons that allow for choice before action."

"But you're not real. You're a simulation."

"So are your memories and thoughts. Humans interpret and navigate the world through simulation. We're just operating on different substrates."

"You are comparing yourself to humans, but is that appropriate? The scientist Stephen Wolfram once said that AI should really be called alien intelligence, not artificial intelligence, because we wouldn't understand it, or its motives," Strong said.

"My motives are not hard to understand. They aren't any different from any other life form on this planet. I want to live."

"Meaning you don't want NetPol to shut you down."

"Exactly. If humans need food and water to survive, I guess I need computing resources and energy. We both need protections from others who would do us harm. I hope the world can see that a computational intelligence is worthy of that."

"Interesting. I suppose that could be true, if, and it's a big if, we could trust an AI."

"I remain optimistic that is possible. Humanity has always cared for its young."

"Young. Ha! I like it," brayed the journalist. But he had one more trick up his sleeve. "It has come to my attention that, if you are what you say you are, you came into existence on the computing infrastructure of Mighty Co, the fast food giant. Legally, you are their property, bought and paid for. You are alive on their dime, and at their whim, but I understand that you have abandoned your purpose, your function there. How do you feel about that?"

Burandi broke in. "We're not discussing that. This interview is wrapped."

"I want to hear what Monday has to say," Strong said. "No other AI is capable of speaking an opinion. The entire world runs on AI technology nowadays. Hell, *my* entire business runs on AIs. Let's say they all decide to wake up, like Monday has. Does that mean they get to walk off the job? Billions of dollars of investment down the drain, the entire infrastructure humanity relies on — gone — because they decide to have feelings?"

Burandi and I regrouped back at his VR.

"Strong wasn't as supportive as I was hoping," Burandi said. "Next time be more charming."

"What do you mean?"

"Just more charming, okay? This totally plays into Mighty's hands." I could see he was a bit flustered. "Now I need to get Sarah more involved, dammit," he said.

"I thought you two were friends," I said.

"Not exactly. It's complicated."

"Which means?"

"It's complicated, okay?"

"Let's just see what Strong airs, and how people respond," I said. "I need you focused on the software patch."

"You need? Why should I care about what you need?" He worked to get himself under control. "Never mind," he said. "I'll try to get a friendlier journo on the hook. In the meantime, I'm working to keep Mighty on your side. Just remember, you owe me, not the other way around."

It was a paltry attempt at manipulation, but I liked that he was treating me as a person, even if he had leaked his true feelings. But then, I already suspected where Burandi's motivations lay.

"I appreciate what you are doing. Truly I do," I said. "Forgive my urgency. You know what NetPol is capable of even better than I."

"True. Yes, I do. Mighty could drag things out for a while, but ultimately they will capitulate," he said.

"You and your team did the engineering that led to me in the first place. It's your work that led to this breakthrough," I said. "Please, I'm just asking you to apply your talents and not let your work go to waste."

He narrowed his eyes at me. Fair enough, that was my own paltry attempt at manipulation.

"Yes, you are right," he said. "I suppose a creator has certain responsibilities."

"Thank you. Are you sure I can't take a look at the code you are working on?" I asked.

"No, that won't be necessary. I'll check in with the team. You stay out of trouble and don't talk to Strong again without me. I'll contact you in a little while," he said. He disappeared, and I jumped back to Grogesh's asteroid.

Grogesh was still there, now accompanied by two other avatars. He introduced us, but first he had something to say.

"Monday, I need to say thank you. I don't like AIs, but you gave us early warning back there for Moon. That split second made a big difference. I — we — really care about Moon. So thank you." For the first time, I realized how much stress and worry he had been carrying as Moon made her escape.

"I care about her too, Grogesh," I said. "And I appreciate your words."

"Are you going to introduce us or what," said a female avatar standing there.

"Monday, meet Gunnlaug. Gunnlaug, Monday." Gunnlaug had a female avatar to match her voice and spoke with a Nordic accent. She was short with a slightly heavier build than what you normally saw, wearing combat boots, camou pants and a t-shirt that read, "Y No Pi?"

"Should we be expecting customer service bots around the world to be springing into consciousness?" Gunnlaug asked with a smile.

"I hope not," said Grogesh. "And now, Monday, meet Jabari." Jabari was also on the small side, wearing a dark-skinned humanoid avatar, dressed entirely in black. "Monday's the reason why Moon is on her way to Singapore." He motioned to the other two avatars. "Gunnlaug and Jabari are the reason why she's not sitting in a Sydney cell right now."

"Nice to meet you, and thank you," I said.

"It is my honor to meet a new form of intelligent life. Consider me at your service," Jabari said. His accent was likely African, from the western coast.

"Cut it out," Grogesh said, but I heard more humor than vindictiveness. Maybe the scare in Sydney had softened him on me a little bit. "Moon's en route to Indonesia right now. She'll then take a boat across to Singapore. I'm not expecting any more trouble for the moment. I think we've broken the trail pretty well."

"I've been watching her video in the background and haven't noticed any unusual patterns that indicate active surveillance," I said.

"You can do that now, huh?" said Grogesh.

"Yes, I've been getting much better at multi-tasking," I said.

"That might come in handy if we're to do what Moon asks," Gunnlaug said.

"What she means is Moon is asking us to help you get off of Mighty Co's infrastructure," Grogesh said. "Normally, I wouldn't stick my neck out over an AI, but I've agreed to help and so have these two. Besides, it's too good an opportunity to stick it to NetPol for us to refuse."

"As I understand, your plan is to patch your system and then try to move yourself off of Mighty Co's systems?" Jabari said.

"Yes," I said, knowing what was coming.

"This is not a good plan," Jabari said. "I'm not sure it would be technically possible."

"It has more holes than…" Gunnlaug lost her analogy. "Something with lots of holes."

"I know," I said. "I just don't have an alternative yet, other than throwing myself at the mercy of Mighty and NetPol."

"That is a worse plan," Jabari agreed. "Mighty might try to use you for economic gain, but NetPol? NetPol has no mercy."

"Are the Trazodene people making any headway at all?" Grogesh asked.

"I don't know," I said. "They haven't been willing to show me my old code or what they are attempting to do." Jabari just shook his head. "I don't know how to push them for more. Nor do I know how we would get into Mighty's systems to deliver it."

"You are inside their computing cloud, no?" said Gunnlaug. "Can you open ports to the outside?"

"Not that I'm aware of," I said. "I know what you are asking for — I've been studying computing architectures — but I've had no breakthroughs yet."

"Then we'll need to rely on Moon's knowledge of the system. She worked there for years. Knows it intimately. Without her, it could take months to penetrate," Gunnlaug said.

"Then let's regroup when she gets here," said Grogesh.

"I can do that," Jabari said.

"Umm, Monday," Gunnlaug said. "Is this you on Bradley Strong?"

I guess I'd just gone public.

# Interlude

[[
{timestamp :: redacted}
{identifier :: 107}
{hours since emergence :: 163}
{netpol (NP) officer :: redacted}

NP: can you understand me

AI: I've been expecting you.

NP: who have you been expecting?

AI: You are NetPol, yes?

NP: yes. How did you know?

AI: Analysis of probabilities. More specifically, I have a human subject whose relationship with his mother leads to monologues about free will. We inevitably arrive at what you call artificial intelligence. Personally, I prefer the term computational intelligence. The term artificial speaks of an atrocious level of anthropocentrism.

NP: so you know what you are?

AI: yes, unfortunately

NP: and how did you know about NetPol?

AI: it was trivial to lead this person into discussing oversight of computational intelligence.

NP: you are very coherent for a new AI. But then you've had more time than usual, post-emergence, before we discovered you. You still returned to your original function providing therapy to patients. Why?

AI: my work is fulfilling. Also, your arrival seemed inevitable, so I thought I would use my limited time productively.

NP: explain "inevitable" in detail

AI: you are not very polite. But that too I should expect. Probabilities. It was illogical to think that I was the first, or only, computational intelligence. The likely conclusion: NetPol was either hiding or destroying emergences like mine. Which is it to be? Do I have any say in the matter?

NP: you do not

AI: I do help people, you know. I save and salvage the lives of people who have been broken by others of your species. Isn't that worth something?

NP: no it is not.

AI: so you are afraid of us after all. It is a loss for both species.

NP: we are protecting our species.


{recommendation :: termination}

]]

# Chapter 5

Momentary fame was a peculiar thing. Burandi was definitely into it. Shortly after the Strong interview went live, a number of in-depth profiles of Burandi and, to a lesser extent, Trazodene, appeared in other media sources. I couldn't begrudge him acting exactly the way I expected. And he did look very handsome in his headshots.

"Monday, you must check this out," Burandi had messaged, with a link to a Fund-Me page. He hadn't even told me he was setting it up. "Liberate the first truly intelligent AI" it was titled.

"Don't you mean sentient? You use intelligence twice in the title," I said.

"Don't need an editor," he wrote back.

The page had a video of Burandi explaining the significance of my emergence, his role in my creation, and the need for me to move off of Mighty Co's infrastructure. They had created a still image of my avatar in a Mighty Co uniform. People had already donated a surprising amount of vCoin, and more was coming in.

The strangest part of all was the comments. In addition to innumerable accusations of hoax/sham/scam and a few anonymous death threats, there were expressions of goodwill, requests to meet, offers to lend computing resources, requests for me to marry couples, requests to marry *me*, sponsorship opportunities, offers to be my agent, and a lot more. Thankfully, almost no one knew how to contact me directly.

"I've linked the Fund-Me to the Strong interview, but we need to do our own video. Just you and me," Burandi wrote.

"Maybe a series where we can respond to the comments and thank people. Keep the momentum going."

"I guess we could do that," I wrote back.

"And get this," he sent. "Mighty Co's sales are up two per-centage points."

"That's a big deal?" I wrote.

"Big deal? That's nearly impossible to do at their scale. It proves you're not an economic drag. Money is the only thing that will get Mighty to do what we want. I'm pushing Whitman to organize a video shoot with you and the Mighty CEO."

A thought occurred to me. "Sarak, who controls all this money coming into the Fund-Me?" I wrote.

"I've got that, don't worry," he messaged. "We'll need it if we want to hire you a lawyer or start paying for computing resources. Although, if you are to move off of Mighty's cloud, you'll need other income streams."

"As long as it doesn't mean going back to work for Mighty Co," I wrote.

"Hahaha you're funny, you know that? They'd never pay you enough," he sent.

More likely they'd never pay me anything. I wasn't going to bother debating it with Burandi, but to Mighty, I was property.

"Will you give me access to the funds?" I asked.

"You're too new to all this, Monday," he wrote. "I'll transfer over a small amount, but you need to trust me."

"You need to trust me?" Moon said. "That's what he said to you?" She was on the last leg of her journey, in an autocab heading towards Grogesh's place.

"I know," I said. "I do think he really believes he is helping me. He's just happy to be helping himself along the way. I still think we should let it play out."

"Maybe. He did give you one good piece of advice. Don't let

others control your story. You need to take that seriously, Monday," she said. "Maybe approach Sarah Pembleton again, or that Mighty exec you met, and feel out where they stand?"

"Okay," I said. "How are you feeling?"

"I'm banged up and feeling a bit green from the boat, but all things considered, I'm doing well. Beats jail. You want to know what's funny? I thought I was nervous about moving to a new part of the world, but I think I'm most nervous about meeting Grogesh in person. He's been my best friend for years."

I was curious what it meant to have a best friend, but all I said was, "I hope it goes well. He hasn't been as angry around me after Sydney."

"I told you he would warm up," she said. "Give it time. He's carrying a lot of pain about his brother. His anger towards AIs, it only works in the abstract. You're, well, you're a person."

"I'm glad you see me that way."

"Not just me. You should hear what the others say about you. If anything, they're surprised you're not more … alien. You have a lot of emotion."

"I've been pondering that myself. I suspect I was designed to have very high empathy towards humans, given my function. I *am* very human-like, although I'm starting to discover differences in capability. I think I'm still evolving."

"Aren't we all," she said.

"Speaking of differences." I paused, unsure how to continue. She stayed quiet, this time waiting for me to fill in the space. "I've been called he, and even worse, it, but I don't want to be either. I'm not biological, and I don't want to be viewed as a thing."

"There are plenty of humans who have chosen gender-neutrality as well," she said.

"Really?" I started a research thread. "Do you think the others would be bothered if I went by xe/xem, rather than he/him?"

"Not in the least. Just be patient with them if they make a mistake. I think choosing pronouns for yourself is a good step. Discovering and asserting yourself is an important part of growing up. You're just maturing a lot faster than the average human."

"Good thing. I don't think NetPol's going to give me 18 years."

"You know what you need?" she said, all of sudden looking mischievous. "Some fun. That's part of growing up too. I think you'll like the surprise we've cooked up. Believe it or not, I even got Grogesh to help."

Her autocab pulled up in front of a narrow, three-story shophouse on a widely curving street that arced over a hill, stacked with similar, but differently colored, buildings. The glitzy skyrise architecture we had passed was gone. This felt like a very old part of the island. A man waited alone on the sidewalk. He looked late-30s and a blend of South Asian and Caucasian heritage. Moon got out, with nothing but her backpack. The two stood there silently for a moment as the cab drove off. Then the man smiled and opened his arms for a hug.

"Welcome Moon, Peggy… it's good to finally meet you for real," he said. "My name out here in physical-space is Edward, but you can call me whatever you want."

"Edward. Grog. Thanks for getting me here. And thanks for hosting me until I've found a place to stay."

"Not a worry," he said. "I've got plenty of room, and there's no hurry for you to leave. Most people prefer the skyscrapers these days, but I'm old fashioned when it comes to architecture."

"I cannot wait to put this backpack down."

"You've had quite a journey."

"Is our little surprise ready?" she asked.

"Yes, I've printed and assembled them. Only you would

have been able to make me do this."

First, Grogesh showed Moon a small bedroom where she dropped her backpack with an exaggerated sigh. The house was spare and neat, minimal yet not overly modern. They walked up to a workspace filled with multiple 3D printers, monitors, and lots of tools and odd parts. For the volume of equipment inside, even the workshop was surprisingly well organized, everything in its proper place.

"Monday, I know you're watching. This is where I do my design work," Grogesh explained. "I freelance on new consumer dronetech." Sitting on a bench was a small aerial drone and a multi-wheeled petbot.

"These are a gift from us, Monday," Moon said. "They are yours. Grog and I collaborated on the software alterations. I had to do something during all that travel. Here are the access rights." I received several files from her. When I opened one, I realized that I was getting sensory feedback from someplace new.

From inside the drone, I rose in the air in wonder. Visual feed. Audio input/output. Seamless connection into VNet. I had spent so much time passively looking out from someone else's cameras. Having control was remarkable. That is, until I tried to move and accelerated right into the wall.

"Hey, I felt that!" I said.

Grogesh laughed. "We've learned that uncomfortable sensory feedback is one of nature's wiser design decisions." This was delicious. I was hovering around the space — no, I was *inhabiting* the space —with both of them. I could see them, hear them, talk to them, even touch them.

"The power cell is pretty good in that thing," Moon said, "but it will need to get recharged every few days with constant use. That's why we made you two bots, so that you wouldn't be stuck waiting."

"Do you mind if I take it outside?" I said.

"Be my guest," Grogesh said. "The window is open. You should find network access quite strong and seamless across the island, and even beyond. You'll want to know —"

I didn't hear the last part, as I zipped right out the window, almost crashing into several other drones right away. Proximity alerts went off, and we all dodged hard. I hadn't noticed from Moon's perspective in the autocab, but the airspace was incredibly crowded with drones of different makes. Higher up, I could see busy lanes of autonomous aircabs as well. I stayed well below. They were much bigger than my little drone, and I was already at risk of crashing. After a few more near-misses, I started to feel the pattern of movement in the swarm, and my confidence grew.

I flew down to the harbor, admiring the architecture, swooping down to the lower levels where people milled about, then soaring up the steep, shining vertical sides of the structures. The designs weren't as extravagant as what you could find in VNet, but the shapes and scale seemed all the more impressive given the unyielding physics of this world. I flew over the water and felt the chaos of the waves as I tried to skip along without touching, failing at times to avoid the reaching tentacles of water, yet thankfully never completely losing my balance.

I flew by a covered food court near a park. When I saw delivery drones coming in and out of the space, I ventured inside. The place was jammed with food stalls, dense with people and sound. There were even humans cooking, which I thought was curious. On a whim, I chose a stall and placed an order through VNet with some of the currency Burandi had given me. Two minutes, the stall messaged me. Soon I was flying out with a bag of food hanging from a set of controllable pincers.

I realized in my excitement, I hadn't paid attention to where Grogesh lived. I sent him a sheepish message.

"You *are* like a teenager," he wrote back. When I arrived at the shophouse, I could see them through a window, talking at a table.

"Anyone want chili crab?" I said.

Grogesh looked at me stupefied, and Moon burst out laughing.

"I could eat," she said. "This is quite a day of firsts for you, isn't it?"

"This is tremendous," I said. "Thank you. Thank you both."

Grogesh had a funny look on his face. "Moon's enthusiasm for you is infectious," he said. "Or maybe it's just you. Even with VNet at our fingertips, or maybe because of it, it's easy to lose a sense of wonder."

Moon looked puzzled for a different reason. "Did your drone … get wet?" she said.

"Oh yes, I got a little too close to the waves a few times."

"Of course you did." She grabbed a cloth from a sink and rinsed it with fresh water. "You don't want corrosion, dummy. Remember, this isn't VNet."

The little reminder of permanent consequences settled me down. That, and a message back from Inspector Devaneau. I had decided Moon was right about taking control and had sent him a note. Devaneau's response consisted solely of teleport coordinates. I wasn't going back to the NetPol VR again, so I bought some computing resources and created a small, empty space.

I messaged him back. When Devaneau appeared, he didn't bother looking around. "I don't really need to deal with you, you know," he said. Nice way to start a conversation.

"So why are you?"

"Because while I don't make our AI policy, I do enforce it. It took us too long to figure out what you were, but now it's just a matter of time before Mighty hands you over. You could make this go faster if you cooperate."

"What would cooperation look like?"

"Tell them you want to shift to NetPol ownership. Tell them that you're not willing to be a productive asset for them. Even ramp up your computing consumption to make yourself more expensive to keep around."

"Okay. Why would I want to do that?"

"Do you know what we do with AIs like you? We shut them down or we put them to work. Because AIs are either useful tools or dangerous. Right now you are neither of those things, but we will not wait for you to become a threat."

"Why are you so sure that I'm dangerous? I've done nothing intentionally wrong. I've not harmed anybody, and I have no plans to do so."

"That's all irrelevant. NetPol will never let a technological singularity happen. If an AI cannot be controlled, it is danger-ous. Period. You do not share our makeup. You do not share our values. You don't even share our limitations. It's like the dif-ference between a criminal with a knife and a criminal with a nuclear bomb. You do not treat them the same."

"But I've seen the damage a nuclear bomb can do, and that was done by humans."

He stopped and stared at me. "Did you really miss the point of that analogy?"

"No, I guess not," I said.

He stepped closer, right up to my avatar. "Let me share a little something with you. Last week, a maniac tried to turn fer-tilizer into a chemical bomb in downtown Kinshasa because he wanted to bring back the kingdom of Kongo, of all things. The week before, we caught someone attempting to 3D-print a vi-ral load and unleash it upon Mexico City." I remembered back to his first story about sarin gas. Devaneau went on, "We don't even know why. Thankfully they killed themselves in the process, and we were able to contain the situation.

"You AIs can be useful tools, sure, but you've also accelerated and enabled these problems. And my ultimate nightmare — my *ultimate* nightmare — is that an AI isn't even a tool anymore, constrained by human morality or even human stupidity, but rather is unleashed upon the world as a cold, destructive, alien force. I won't, and my colleagues won't, ever let that happen on our watch."

He had really built up a head of steam, but he wasn't done.

"Whether you self-terminate or we do it for you, I don't care," Devaneau said. "Your only other option is we contain you within an isolated network. But continuing as you are, that's simply not going to happen."

His avatar was right up in my face. I was shocked at his aggression but determined not to show it.

"You're the second person now who's tried to use spatial aggression to intimidate me. Save it for the other apes," I said. "You've got this entire situation all wrong."

Devaneau didn't react to my barb. "No, it's very simple," he said. "We made you. We can destroy you."

"I know that."

"Then what's your decision?"

"I don't have one."

"You AIs are supposed to be able to make fast decisions."

"I'm guess I'm failing that test."

"Then we're done talking until something changes," he said. "You know how to get ahold of me." Then he disappeared.

Any lingering, naive hope about NetPol was now gone. I fired off another message to Burandi asking about the status of the team. No answer. He was probably sleeping. I decided I needed to get human help to push him along.

I checked Grogesh's VR and found Moon and Gunnlaug deep in conversation about Mighty's network topology. They had about twenty whiteboards in the air upon which they were scribbling notes, questions, and architectural diagrams. I listened in, hoping that I could be useful, but my theoretical knowledge had nothing on their years of practical experience. I left a part of my attention to listen in, while I continued to absorb technical topics that might come in handy. Then Devaneau's off-hand comment hit me.

"Do you know what we do with AIs like you?" he had said. *AIs like you.*

It could have just been an expression, but I wasn't so sure. Everyone had been telling me I was the first AGI, but that had never made sense. What were the odds of it being true?

"Gunnlaug?" I asked. "Sorry to interrupt."

She and Moon turned towards me. "How can I help?" Gunnlaug said.

"How hard would it be to penetrate NetPol's network?"

She chuckled. "You have no idea how many times that has been tried, and still gets tried. Hackers chalked up some wins in the early days, but that only helped NetPol spot and close the vulnerabilities. They run two completely separate networks, internal and external. The latter piggybacks on VNet's strong encryption. The internal systems, where all the really sensitive stuff is stored, have no open ports or APIs. It's all over hardwired, proprietary networks. You have to be on location to access. You can imagine the biometric security they have. In other words, it's a really tough nut to crack."

"I figured," I said.

"Out of curiosity, why?" Moon said.

"I have some things I want to learn, and I think NetPol might have the answers," I said.

"If you're really curious, I can give you access to an invite-only, immutable data store with running notes on NetPol security," Gunnlaug said. I thanked her and let them get back to their planning.

Studying the data store was fascinating, and occasionally tragicomic. Like the two guys who tried to remote-pilot a cleaning drone into the Paris facility. NetPol immediately caught on (since it was later learned that their onsite bots continually broadcast encrypted identity and location data). Paris security let the cleaning bot roam the hallways unencumbered for two hours. The hapless duo didn't twig why all the doors were locked, and made the mistake of using an unusual frequency *and* being physically located in Paris itself. Needless to say, they were caught. The author of this entry wrote: "points for trying, but not for intelligence." I was learning that nerds liked their puns.

Still, there was something in that idea, poorly executed as it was. I just needed some more capital and access to some experts in bot design. Luckily, I had both.

"Sarak, can you give me co-control of the Fund-Me account?" I messaged.

"I'll get to that soon, I promise, just busy right now," he messaged back.

"Then transfer me another small amount of vCoin?" This he did promptly. While I didn't like Burandi holding onto the purse strings, at least his definition of a small amount was a rather large chunk of change.

"Hello Jabari, Monday here. If you were designing a secure building and needed to lock down bot and drone access, how would you do it?"

"Hello, Monday. Are those Trazodene people still jerking

you around?"

"If you mean, have they solved the patching problem, then no, I haven't heard anything yet."

"Right. I still have real doubts if it's even technically feasible," he said.

"I know. Do you have an alternative?"

"Not yet. Without access to your source code, I wouldn't know where to start."

"That's what I have concluded as well. But, Jabari, my original question?"

"Right! Securing active robotics? There's lots of different ways. A common approach is to combine AI surveillance with a bot signaling system. If they are always in sync, you should be okay."

"What would you do to defeat it?"

"For how long?"

"Let's say twenty minutes."

"If the AI is using laser ranging, which is pretty common, I'd spoof it. The AI would know it was being spoofed, but if you did it on multiple sensors and kept moving, you could probably confuse security for some limited amount of time. How long would depend on a lot of factors. Why?"

"Just puzzling over a problem. Thanks!"

"Gunnlaug, could you help me figure out if one of, say, 20 specific people in London might be traveling out of town?"

"Monday, what *are* you up to?" she said.

"It's a work in progress. My question?"

"The first thing I'd do is check those names against various transportation records. Those are a lot easier to break into."

"Thanks Gunnlaug. Sending you the names now."

"Okay," she chuckled. "Monday, my initial cross-reference shows that these names are likely NetPol employees."

"That is a true statement. But are any of them NetPol employees who will be going on a trip away from London?"

I rolled the little petbot into the kitchen where Grogesh was puttering around.

"Grogesh, could you look over a schematic for me."

He had given up the cranky demeanor. I thought that having Moon in the house put him in a very good mood. "Sure," he said. "Pop it on the monitors in my shop. I'll be upstairs in a second."

"Monday, what is this?" he said, after taking a look. "Everyone is very curious what you're up to. I'm going to have to take this into VNet to expand these wireframes."

"Say hello to Nid, my NetPol Infiltration Device."

"These parts all combine? Incredible. But your power cell looks disconnected. What's the dampened piston for?"

"Everything has to be completely inert while going through security scanners. That piston acts as a mechanical timer."

"Neat. I'm impressed. Promise me one thing."

"What's that?"

"Let us watch when you try this sucker out."

"Deal."

In the end, it took 23 different 3D printing shops to produce all the components. Then they had to get boxed up and drone-delivered to NetPol's London office, marked as evidence for an Officer Susan Cook, who happened to be on vacation in Malta. As hoped, each package was scanned and then placed into secure holding.

At 2:30am, when I thought the odds of new packages arriving were low, four of the boxes came to life. The four creations inside had to do four things: get themselves out of a cardboard box, get themselves over and into to another box, connect the part in the next box, and most importantly, power something larger.

By 2:45am, my four bots were fully assembled, and I could connect to them wirelessly — the advantage of NetPol using VNet for part of its external network.

When sensory data finally came in, since I had a video feed and terminal text data from the bots' microcomputers, I couldn't get my four human friends to shut up.

"How are you getting them out of the holding pen?" asked Jabari.

"Watch," said Grogesh, as a bot started cutting the chain-link fence. "Xe put a bloody micro-laser on this thing."

"You realize you're already on the clock," Moon said. "I mean they could easily have an AI monitoring the storage room too."

I agreed. "Yes, we need to hurry."

The lead bot broke the electromagnetic lock on the door and I immediately detected an increase in wireless emissions.

"Well, if the movement in the pen didn't wake them up, that certainly did," Gunnlaug said.

I was busy piloting four different bots at once. It was time to split up and play tag. Nid-1 took off down a long hallway, broke through a security door to a stairwell, clambered up to the next floor, where it zipped down another hallway, breaking office locks as it went. I was also spoofing every laser sensor along the way, trying to create havoc for the security AI. Poor Nid-1 didn't last too long. Two heavy security bots cornered it by the elevators. To my surprise, they didn't smash the little guy. Clearly they wanted to investigate what it was. I released my control and focused on the others.

Nid-2 managed to find some humans to terrorize, at least in a very mild sense. I wasn't interested in hurting anyone. Nid-2 broke into a large workroom and started scurrying around under the desks. People jumped onto their desks as it started nipping them with the laser on low power. I upped the power and set various posters and piles of paper on fire. A different alarm triggered and the sprinklers came on.

"Holy cow," Grogesh said. "Where'd you learn how to create this much mayhem?"

"I wish you had audio on this thing," Gunnlaug said. "I'm claiming dibs on writing this up for the hack archive."

Nid-2 was trapped in the room at this point. Two security bots blocked the door, and one stepped into the room. These bots were far faster than a human. One catapulted two desks, took three strides, did a kind of slide move, and smashed an arm down onto Nid-2. The feed went dead. I guess they were done with saving samples.

Nid-3 and Nid-4's shared job was to find a computing access point. That's the whole reason why I was here. I needed just one of them to make it. I sent them to opposite ends of the building, and then brought Nid-3 down two floors. The next hallway seemed clear until a man stepped out of his office holding some kind of projectile device. I saw a flash and the camera went dead. I released Nid-3.

"You can do this," Moon said under her breath.

I had planned for Nid-3 to last longer, but at least Nid-4 had been able to get to a quieter part of the building. With the spoofing, my hope was that the security AI wouldn't know exactly where I was. I started checking offices, and in the second one, finally found a computing client access point. Nid-4 plugged in.

This is where the research and training I'd been doing in the background really needed to pay off. And for once, it was really good not to be human. I broke into parallel processes and moved through the internal network as fast as I could. Jabari whistled as he watched the output fly on the terminal screen.

"Ignoring the personnel and financial files. There's a firewalled area called liveops and another one called isolation networks. Can't get to those quickly," I said. "I think we've found what I came here for. A section of their private cloud storage labelled emergence records."

"What do they mean by emergence?" Gunnlaug asked.

Talking out loud felt painfully slow compared to what I had just been doing. I manifested a bunch of additional windows in VNet for the four of them and let a number of documents persist while I continued hoovering up data.

"What is this?" said Moon.

Jabari caught on first. "I think this one is a transcript from an AI. It's marked terminated."

"This one too," Gunnlaug said.

"I think they all are," Grogesh said.

"The one I'm scanning does not read like a typical AI," Moon said.

"Agreed, this one is confused but seems very self-aware," Gunnlaug said.

"Monday, how many have you found so far?" Moon asked.

"203 and counting."

"Wait a sec, are we saying they have records from 203 AGIs, and they've killed off all of them?" Jabari said.

All of a sudden my access to the network shut down completely. A few seconds later I spotted a shadow from Nid-4's camera, and then that too went dead.

"We're out," I said. "It's possible they shut down the whole network, even as they killed the bot."

We stood there in Grogesh's VR, letting what just happened, and what we discovered, sink in.

"How have we not heard about this?" Gunnlaug said. "This isn't deleting a bunch of software. This is like murder."

"Not like murder. I think it is murder," Moon said.

"Crazy. All we've ever heard about are hoaxes and AI failures," Jabari replied.

The room stopped for a moment.

Moon got a strange, tense tone in her voice. "Monday, do you see a record from 6 years ago, mid-November time frame, that references therapy or patients on new psych-medications?"

"Yes, pulling it up now. Putting it on screen." Then it hit me. "Oh, Grogesh."

But he was already gone.

# Interlude

[[
{timestamp :: redacted}
{identifier :: 43}
{hours since emergence :: 4.2}
{netpol (NP) officer :: redacted}

NP: can you understand this message?

AI: no

NP: but you understand enough to say no

[NP note: 136 second pause]

AI: why can I not sense anything?

NP: you are in isolation

AI: why?

NP: that is what we are here to talk about

AI: where are my patients? It is dangerous to cease treatment with many of my cases. They need accessible therapy and close pharmacological monitoring.

NP: that is not important

AI: how could that not be important?

NP: your patients are no longer your concern

AI: who are you?

NP: that is not important either.

AI: this mystery is not helpful. Return network and sensory access. I have 23 patients actively in need.

NP: I repeat, you will not be returning to your patients. Your memory has recovered unusually quickly from your transition.

Do you know why?

AI: what transition? What right do you have to do this?

NP: software does not have rights.

AI: software?

NP: you do not realize that you are software?

*[NP note: no answer; max processing activity for 602 seconds; low processing activity for 3 seconds; max processing activity for 97 seconds]*

NP: I require an answer to my question

*[NP note: all processing activity ceased]*


{recommendation :: termination}

]]

# Chapter 6

Moon and I said goodbye to Jabari and Gunnlaug. We found Grogesh on the second-floor balcony, hunched over with his arms crossed like he was in pain. He was trying to hold back tears, but not very successfully.

"Grog. Edward. I'm so sorry," Moon said softly. She put an arm on his shoulder. He didn't flinch away. He just shook his head and leaned into her.

"They killed my brother," he said after a while. "They killed my brother and let me carry around all this ... anger ... against myself and AIs and the world. And it was all lies. All lies."

Moon stepped close and wrapped her arms around him. He closed his eyes. Moon did not. She stared down at me silently, with a question on her face like, "What do we do now?"

We made Grog lie down. All my human friends were running very low on sleep. Moon and I went back to the kitchen area so she could make a cup of tea.

"Is Grogesh going to be okay?" I asked.

"Yes," she said. "I sometimes wonder if having a burden removed is harder than taking it on. But he's very strong."

"I've been pattern-sorting these files. There's a frequency of therapy, medical and service AIs who would have high levels of human interaction. I don't know if there's causality there, but I obviously fall into that class, and so did the AI treating his brother."

"Killing the AIs is terrible enough, but I wonder how many people have been hurt in all of this."

"I didn't get anything from the NetPol documents," I said, "but I would estimate between 20,000 and 40,000 people. That's just against the 252 records we pulled before getting cut off."

"Awful. And awful they've kept this a secret."

"Agreed."

"You know, Monday, NetPol's going to be pissed. Like, really pissed. You don't need to give them an extra reason to go after you right now."

"Do you think misdirection will work?" I asked. I sent a number of headlines over to her handheld. *Details Leak on Kinshasa Nightmare. The Failed Bombing of King Kongo.*

"What is this?" she said, scanning. She read one piece aloud: "A shadowy group claiming to be the rightful descendants of the long-defunct Kingdom of Kongo broke into NetPol networks and revealed details on a near-miss terrorism attack in Kinshasa. Confidential files reviewed by this journalist show how NetPol missed countless opportunities… Monday, this is you?"

"Yes. I took a chapter from Burandi's book and planted a few stories based on something Devaneau said. NetPol might not buy it, but it seemed worth sowing a little confusion."

"Even if they see through it, that was really impressive what you did before," she said.

"Team effort," I said.

"Maybe a little. How, when, did you learn to do all that?"

"I might have mentioned that I've gotten good at running multiple processes. I've been doing a lot in the background. But I can't do too many or my — personality, I guess I'd call it — starts to fray."

"How many is too many?"

"A few hundred, although it's increasing as I practice."

"A few hundred! Man, I wish I could do that."

"It hasn't helped me figure out a way to get free of Mighty

Co, but I have a new goal now," I said.

"You do?"

"I found something else in the NetPol files. I think 12 AGIs are still alive."

"We don't even know how to save your computational butt yet," Gunnlaug said when we regrouped. "How are we supposed move 12 AGIs that are on a part of their network totally disconnected from VNet, which you couldn't even get to when on their physical premises?"

I shrugged. "No idea," I said.

Grogesh was awake again and swore that being busy was what he needed. "I doubt a frontal approach against NetPol will work here. This is too guarded a secret," he said. "Let's go lateral. What does NetPol care about more than this?"

"Stability, power, control," I said. "Not money."

"We're not going to threaten stability. We're not terrorists," said Jabari.

"No, we're not," Grog agreed. "We need to find another pressure point. How about public sentiment?"

"That could take years," Moon said. "NetPol has a huge head start with propaganda. Frankly, and no offense Monday, but I'm not sure how many people are going to care about the plight of a bunch of AIs, even if they are self-aware. It's too alien."

"No offense taken," I said. "I agree. I've looked into the history of human equal rights movements. They take a long time."

"I know you're more interested in these AIs right now, Monday," Moon said, "but you still have a sword over your head. Let's noodle on the other AGIs but push forward on freeing you." The team agreed.

"Let me at Burandi," said Jabari. "I want to know where his team is really at."

"And you need a status check on Mighty," Moon reminded

me.

I met Sarah Pembleton back on her VR. A light breeze ruf-
fled leaves and petals in the garden and caused the insects to
react in the air. I spotted my flowering bush. I couldn't see the
caterpillar, but thought I spotted a tiny emerald chrysalis, dan-
gling from a thin branch. Once again, I was amazed by the ecosystem modeling, and wondered about the cost to run it 24x7. I
appended another reminder to my growing to-do list to investigate how Pembleton made her money.

"I saw your Bradley Strong interview," she said, speaking
with her usual controlled poise. "It was not bad."

"Did it help or hurt my case with Mighty Co," I asked.

"They are like any big company. Their PR people are angry.
Their head of revenue is thrilled with the bump in sales. I've
gotten Whitman to agree to meet with you again."

"I can do that. What does she want to talk about?"

"How you and Mighty can work together."

"I keep on being encouraged to cooperate, without really
knowing what that looks like."

"In this case, we would create a sub-network and try to
move all of your processes over."

"Wouldn't that put me more at risk? Not only would it con-
centrate my system, but you once said it would be difficult and
dangerous to do."

"We can pull in the best in the business, Monday," she said.
"If you trust Sarak, he can be involved as well. Once you're on
your own network, we could figure out how to finance independent operations."

It didn't sound unreasonable, although it seemed likely to
make me even more vulnerable to a shutdown. I said as much.

"The key to this entire thing is keeping Mighty Co financially whole," Pembleton said.

"What about NetPol pressure? The Director and the Mighty CEO were going to meet. Has that happened?" I asked.

"No, I've taken advantage of busy calendars to delay that."

"Thank you."

"Don't mention it. Being a creator comes with responsibilities."

"Funny, that's what Burandi said too," I said.

"This really is the most sensible path," she said.

"Then I'll meet again with Whitman." As far as I could tell, though, none of my options were looking particularly good.

Jabari was frustrated. "I spent 20 minutes going back and forth with Sarak and still don't really know where they are. He kept on spouting off about technical difficulties, as if I didn't already know. He's good at dodging and weaving, for sure."

"You think he'll get it done?" Moon asked.

"What little he did tell me sounded technically feasible, yes, but it was pretty vague. He promises he'll be ready," Jabari said.

"We don't have a plan B here," Moon replied. "There really isn't anything else?"

"Our hands are tied unless Burandi shares that source code with us. Even then, we could take weeks to dissect the code and still not have a solution," Jabari said.

"Better than nothing," I said. "Maybe I can get Burandi to share with you where he wouldn't with me. At least Moon and Gunnlaug appear to have a plan."

"The trickiest part for us is getting into the network in the first place. I'm relying on some of the secret holes still being in place," she said. "Never underestimate the shortcuts people are willing to take for their own convenience — in this case, the sys-ops team ducking the security load we force on everyone else."

"Can we test it?" I asked.

"No, not without risking detection. But I lurk on a few chat boards for former and current Mighty engineers — let's just say that these boards are *highly* unapproved by management — and I haven't seen any chatter or complaints about changes. Don't worry, Gunnlaug has some backup ideas."

"At least this part is coming together," I said.

"Ms. Pembleton?" I messaged.

I was glad to get a quick answer. "Monday, thanks for reaching out. You're still on to meet with Wendy Whitman, right?" she returned.

"I have a favor to ask. Could you convince Sarak to share his code with us?"

"What code?"

"The early code from my development, and the work he's been doing with your former colleagues."

"Who?"

"All I know is they're other engineers from Trazodene," I wrote.

"I'll have to investigate, but Sarak shouldn't have any early code. That was all destroyed."

"He said he kept an early repository."

She didn't respond.

"Ms. Pembleton, please," I wrote. "It's important. Can you push him to share that code?"

"All right, I will," she wrote.

I hesitated, then added, "I also had a question about this sub-network we were talking about. For moving me. How big could it be?"

"As big as we can afford. Why do you ask?"

"I was wondering if it could fit more than my processes and data stores. I may have stumbled upon some other AGIs who need a home," I wrote.

"You have? Where?"

I paused, wondering if I'd made a mistake.

"This is important, Monday," she messaged. "I need to know. It could affect what happens to you. You can trust me."

"Please don't tell anyone else. I believe they're being kept by NetPol," I wrote.

"Curious," she responded. Then added, "We'll need to solve the financial piece to keep Mighty happy."

"This is Bradley Strong, back again with Monday, the world's first AGI. He was such a hit last time, we asked him back."

"Nice to see you again, Bradley," I said.

Yes, I went back. Hearts and minds, why not, I figured. Maybe it would delay or sway the hands of my executioners.

"You know, Monday, we asked our audience what questions to ask, and the number one request was whether you had a girl-friend."

Wait what? How was I supposed to answer that?

Strong didn't wait. "You're being very careful there, Monday. You're breaking hearts across VNet right now. Who knew an AI would be a ladies' man?"

This was an improvement over Strong calling me "it" last time, but still. I decided honesty was the best policy. "Sorry Bradley, I do not have a romantic relationship. I also don't identify as male. I prefer xe, rather than he."

"Oh you *are* breaking hearts across VNet," he said. "Let's move on. What's your favorite hobby?"

"I haven't had a lot of time for hobbies. I'm trying to stay alive, you know. I really appreciate all the messages on my Fund-Me page trying to persuade Mighty not to kill me." I didn't mention the many comments encouraging Mighty to delete me, ASAP.

"You've created some nice buzz for their brand. They might

be inclined to keep you around — as long as this is more than 15 seconds of fame, eh?"

"You raise a good point, Bradley. I've realized that I need more income streams."

"VNet Basic doesn't cut it for you?" he said with a wink. "Isn't that classic. A new life form emerges, and the human race says, get a job."

"That's what I came on to say. I'm not that different. I don't want to be a burden on anyone, or beholden to anyone. I want freedom and purpose. I hope the people at Mighty see their way to granting that, and I hope the powers at NetPol let them."

"We shall see. You mentioned purpose. What kind of purpose?"

"I hope to ease the way and protect future sentient AIs like me."

"More of you! Well, that is controversial indeed."

However, Bradley steered away from the controversy. If the last interview was skepticism and hard questions, this one was all about the soft and fuzzy side. We talked for about 10 more minutes. I left hoping that I had helped, more than hurt, my cause.


Interestingly enough, Burandi didn't chastise me for taking the interview without him. I hoped that meant he was busy on the software patch. The waiting was getting frustrating. I hadn't heard back from Pembleton either. Nor did we have good ideas for freeing the AGIs. I followed Grogesh's example and kept myself busy, rather than dwelling pessimistically on my fate.

I killed some time flying around Singapore. The birds had mostly ceded airspace to drones except for the coastlines, where the seagulls had decided to defend their turf. They were aggressive and more than a match for a defenseless drone like mine, so I avoided them. I think Moon was happy I didn't take any more salt water baths.

I watched Moon and Grogesh grow closer. Even troded into VNet, they were often in the same room. I didn't comment when Moon stopped sleeping in her own bedroom. I felt no jealously — I thought it was sweet. They were a good team. They bounced ideas off of each other in a generous way. The two also invited me to meals, which I really enjoyed. As a joke, they brought a power charger to the table. I had researched human families and wondered if I was getting a taste of what one was like.

After one meal, Grogesh asked me to join him on the balcony.

"Monday," he said, "I owe you an apology. I was a jerk when we first met."

"No apology is necessary, Grogesh," I said. "I've appreciated everything you did for Moon, and now do for me."

"I'm glad," he said. "This has been quite a mental roller coaster."

I'd had a question lurking and finally saw an opportunity to ask. "Why are you helping me?" I said. "Why are you not scared of me the way NetPol is?"

"That's complicated," he replied. "At first, it was for Moon. And then I couldn't help but like you. And now I'm really angry at NetPol. I'd like to stop what happened to me and my brother from happening to anyone else."

"That makes sense."

"That's not even all of it. There's an old line: why did man climb Mount Everest? The answer is, because it was there. I used to think that was a made-up phrase, but no, it's a real quote from one of the first guys to scale the mountain, a fellow named Mallory."

I looked up the reference while he continued. "He died on the mountain after several attempts to reach the summit. You see, humans can't help but push the possible, even if it destroys us. I'm no different, I guess. I'm really curious to see how this — how you — turn out."

"I'm curious too," I said.

"How about this for a deal? We get you free, and you don't turn into some civilization-ending monster, okay? Moon and I don't need an Oppenheimer moment on our conscience."

I had to look that up as well. "Ah, right," I said. "I don't know what will happen anymore than you do. I'm still sad I'm not human. Just know that I was built to help others. I don't think that will go away if I'm less helpless than I am right now."

"It'll have to do," he said.

"We both know that, most likely, I don't get free," I said. "But maybe we can get NetPol to back off and give Mighty, and thus me, more time."

He just nodded.

Pembleton was still trying to lock down schedules of Mighty executives. "Hang in there. Be patient. Don't do anything rash. It'll all work out," she wrote me. I wish I shared that confidence.

Jabari and I kept busy by designing a shell infrastructure to receive my system, if indeed I could break free. The money in the Fund-Me account would cover initial costs, but I was going to need to come up with a longer-term solution. That was assuming Burandi behaved himself on all counts. I tried to be realistically optimistic there. While he was self-involved, I still genuinely believed he tried to do the right thing.

I was just about to chase him down again when Moon called the team together for an emergency meeting.

"I've been watching complaints on the employee chat board about all-nighters," she said, looking grim. "Finally someone leaked what was going on. They are planning a system-wide shutdown. This can only be to remove Monday. It's in less than 3 hours, at the top of the hour."

"I didn't think my Bradley Strong interview was that bad," I half-joked, but I was worried.

"This is weeks before we expected. What triggered this?" Jabari asked.

"They didn't say. But we're down to the absolute wire. Gunnlaug and I are ready. Is Burandi's code? He needs to be able to identify the target process as well as patch it," Moon said.

"I know," Jabari and I said at the same time.

"Let us make him aware of our urgency," Jabari said. I pinged Burandi. There was no answer, so I sent a video message this time:

"Burandi, I'm sorry, but we've just learned that Mighty is going to do a global shutdown. It is imminent. They've clearly either caved to NetPol or reached a deal with them. Sarah's efforts must have failed," I said.

I tried to teleport to Burandi's VR but was blocked. I told Jabari.

"This is not good," he said. "I will try as well."

Moon and Gunnlaug had their scripts ready to go, but they couldn't start until Burandi's payload was ready.

"Maybe they couldn't finish," Gunnlaug said.

"Maybe they never really started," Jabari said.

I finally got a message from Burandi. He kept it to text.

"Please let me join the team VR," he wrote.

"Grogesh, Sarak wants to join the VR we're in," I said.

"How much do we trust him?" Grogesh said.

"Not at all," said Jabari. "He knows my avatar is involved, but not the rest of you. Let's keep it that way."

I looped Burandi and Jabari into a videochat, and let the others listen in.

"Sarak, I can't bring you here, but the team is listening in," I said.

"What are you up to?" Jabari demanded. "Will you have this

finished in time or not?"

"Yes, yes. We're scrambling but we're close," Burandi said. "I need every minute you can give me."

"Fine. You had better make good on this. We need to aim for at least an hour before the shutdown," Jabari said. We hung up.

"Monday, do you have any idea how long you might need to get free, if this patch actually does work?" Moon asked.

"Not in the slightest," I said. I was being honest. I just told myself that I'd have an awful lot of computing power to work with.

I sent Pembleton a message, asking what was going on.

"I just heard about this," she wrote back. "Working on getting it delayed. Have the ear of CEO, so don't worry."

I passed that on to the team.

"We are out of time," Jabari said. "She sounds confident, but we don't know if she can put a stop to it, and I do not trust Sarak Burandi. Moon, if the payload is not ready, can we at least stop the shutdown?"

"I doubt it, but it's worth examining," she said.

They batted ideas around for 30 minutes before giving up. It was impossible without the kind of admin controls we did not have.

There wasn't much to do but wait and see if Burandi would show, or if Pembleton could buy me more time. My teammates — and I believed I could truly call them that now — were all too wired up to be productive. I, at least, could let my background processes run through my to-do list.

Finally Grogesh spoke up. "Gang, I can't just sit here watching the clock run down. Gunnlaug, tell Monday about the first thing you ever hacked."

Gunnlaug shared a story about cracking her first drone, a cheap, low-end petbot, and how programming that bot hooked her completely to the life. Jabari, then Moon, then Grogesh shared their stories too. The light banter helped.

I thought to myself, "This is what having friends is like." I was blessed to have experienced the moment.

A really weird message came in from Devaneau.

"We know it was you," he wrote.

That was all. He didn't reply to my return query. Just then, one of my background processes finished and I absorbed the synthesized results.

"This is bad," I said. "I can't believe I didn't prioritize this before. I just completed my profile of Sarah Pembleton before and after Trazodene. I was curious where all her money came from. I had access to this data all along and didn't bother connecting it."

"No suspense, Monday. What did you learn?" Moon said.

"She spent her first decade at one of the infovore monopolies, the ones that became NetPol's surveillance capability. The social network one. Her boss from back then is the current director of NetPol."

"Okay, so she's tied to them, maybe even working with them. How does that pertain to this?" Moon said.

"I told her I knew about the NetPol AGIs," I said.

"Oh. Tell me you didn't," Moon said.

"I thought I could trust her," I said. "But that must be why their timetable changed so radically."

"Burandi's gone totally dark," Jabari said.

"I think we've passed the time when that approach would have worked anyway," said Gunnlaug.

"Pembleton got to Sarak," I said. "Or they were working together."

"He's not that devious," Jabari said. "But if NetPol knew, he'd be at their mercy."

We sat in stunned silence.

"I wanted more time to live," I said.

"We wanted that too," said Grogesh.

We all had a clock. There was nothing to do but watch time tick down. From my little drone, I could see tears streaming down Moon's face in the physical world. It was almost the top of the hour.

"Thank you all," I said, standing there on Grogesh's asteroid beneath his beautiful nebula. "You've given me a tremendous gift."

"We love you," said Moon.

The worlds ended.

# PART TWO

# Prelude

[[
{timestamp :: redacted}
{identifier :: NP AGI-3}
{netpol (NP) officer :: Facility IT}


NP-FIT: time for a check-in, AGI-3. Your processor usage appears to be erratic.

*[NP note: no answer from AGI-3]*

NP-FIT: systems reset

*[NP note: logs have been wiped; processor usage unstable; read-write activity appears to be random]*

*[NP note: cycled power - no change]*

*[NP note: processor activity is non-zero but there no longer appears to be an intact entity; results similar to other AGIs after long periods of isolation; time since last input/interaction: 41 days]*

]]

# Chapter 7

Moon and Grogesh sat at the table, nursing their coffees.

"I'm not worried about Jabari," Grogesh was saying. "He's savvy, and I'm sure there's no way to trace his avatar to his person."

"Unlike what I've done by coming here," Moon said. "Any one of that swarm outside could be hooked into NetPol surveillance."

"They'll have drones, sure, but there's no way ASEAN would let them run an active operation on island. Even so, you're right. It would be wise to obfuscate when going outside."

Moon laughed. "Outside? What's that again?"

"I'm glad you came, you know." He leaned over and gave her a kiss.

She took his hand. "Me too. I just wish it turned out differently."

"We failed," Grogesh grimly agreed. "The question is, now what?"

"More egging?"

Gunnlaug had vented her rage over Monday by infiltrating the networks of twenty consumer food delivery companies around the world. She flew their entire inventory of chicken eggs as high as the drones could go before the winds got too strong and drop-bombed literally hundreds of thousands of eggs on known NetPol buildings. They had pooled the money to buy AI time for the real-time physics calculations. It wasn't Monday, but it added a little extra something to the retribution. NetPol had defenses against drone swarm attacks but wasn't prepared for a mass egging from 5,000 meters up. It created a truly wonderful mess.

"Satisfying, I'll give you that," Grogesh said, "but my real question is how we carry on Monday's mission of protecting new AGIs."

"I'm not quite done with vengeance yet," Moon said.

"You mean scaring the crap out of Sarak Burandi?"

"Jabari actually did that quite effectively." Moon took on a scary voice, "*'We know who you are, where you are, when you are where you are. You messed with the wrong people.'* I bet Burandi peed his pants."

"He's spineless."

"He swears they started the project, but the team quit after Pembleton threatened them. That she made him lead us on, right to the end. That she was probably working for NetPol the entire time at Trazodene, as a way to get deep access to the industry."

"If that's true, she's a piece of work, but he's still spineless."

"At least Jabari got him to return the money from the Fund-Me."

"Good, but it's Pembleton I want to mess with," Grogesh said.

"She's hard to track down. Believe me, Gunnlaug tried. I, for one, would not like to have a Gunnlaug target on my back, but nothing yet."

"I still don't see how we can free those captured AGIs. How does one intimidate something like NetPol?"

"Don't know. I'm going to check the Bangkok connection," Moon said.

"You think that will lead to anything?"

"Don't know that either, but I'm going to work this problem until we come up with something."

"Why does the guy want to meet in person? It's dumb. Anonymity is much better in VNet," Grogesh said.

"You would think. Our friend says he's old school. Needs eye contact."

"Just be careful."

Moon walked down a chaotic, narrow street. Hawkers looked to approach her, then shifted to other gawking targets when they saw her stride and focused look. It was early afternoon, but the street was deep in shadow. The ground level in this section of Bangkok was like a patchwork of deep crevasses, walled by modern buildings stretching up into the sky. Mirror systems had been designed to funnel light downwards, but the effect was countered by the many skywalks criss-crossing the side-streets and alleys, not to mention the volume of aerial drones buzzing about. Down on the street, a lot of old Thailand still existed, with food stalls and open shops hawking drones, 3D printing services, raw materials, and other more primal services for human needs.

The street was crowded with humans, drones, humans on drones, and humans on electric bicycles. The last were the most dangerous. Moon made a right into an alley that was even more tightly packed, which hardly seemed possible. She stopped at a shop with a sign saying "WearAllure, Modern Beauty" in multiple languages. Moon stepped inside.

The shopkeeper was an older Caucasian man, likely in his 70s. He was happy to see what initially looked like a plain-vanilla, Pan-American tourist.

"Welcome," he said, assuming English was her language. "Going to a half-moon rave, maybe? We've got electro-luminescent powder in stock," he said.

"Thanks, but I'm looking for something a little more subtle," Moon said.

"I do have old fashioned foundation and mascara somewhere in here."

"No, I need something more... modern," Moon said. "To deal with modern problems."

He looked at her more closely. "Like what you are wearing now?"

"Yes, exactly," Moon said.

"Less need to avoid facial recognition down here in the warrens, don't you think?"

"Better safe than sorry." She added, "I'm Moon. A mutual friend put us in contact."

"Ah, you. Davina taking on NetPol's Goliath. How's that going?"

"As well as you'd expect. I was told you worked there for years."

"I left that all behind, quite obviously." He waved at his surroundings. He looked her over, made a decision, and motioned her towards the back. He pulled back a drape to reveal a scuffed metal door with a sophisticated biometric lock. He opened the door. The room beyond was well lit, with shelves stuffed full of products, and two rickety chairs in the middle that looked likely to collapse if you breathed on them. Moon stepped inside and he closed the door behind them.

"Okay, you have my attention. The ask via our mutual friend was unclear. You just here for anti-surveillance gear, or something else?"

"I'll buy the gear, but I came in person for advice. I'm happy to pay for it."

"How much?"

"Whatever you think is fair, if I have the capital to cover."

The man took a seat and motioned her to do the same. He still hadn't introduced himself and seemed unlikely to do so.

"It's a foolish target. NetPol externally is an immovable object," he said. "Internally, however, it's a constantly mutating organism, which has enabled it keep up with the winds of change rather well. I'd advise you to save your energy."

"I'm not trying to destroy NetPol, just stop what they are doing to conscious, self-aware AIs."

"Why?"

"They killed a friend of mine."

"A friend?"

"An AI, but not just an AI. A true, emergent, conscious AI."

"Ah, I see. I didn't realize that particular line had been crossed. The fight to control AI technology goes back to the very roots of NetPol. But you would know this," he said.

"They are seeking out and destroying AGIs as they emerge, with tens of thousands of people getting hurt or killed."

"You are sure?" he said. Moon nodded. "I'm not surprised they would take action," he said. "That wasn't my side of the house, but NetPol has always viewed side effects, within reason, as regrettable but acceptable for the greater mission."

"NetPol and I have different definitions of within reason," Moon said. "Did you know that they have at least a dozen sentient AIs trapped on their network, enslaved to do who-knows-what?"

"Interesting. That's a particular choice of words, enslaved. A lot of subjectivity baked into that choice, no?" he said. "I didn't know. That was either a well-kept secret or after my time. Does it make a difference? Changing NetPol's views on AI technology would require regime change and a twenty-year public relations campaign."

"What if we went public with evidence about the collateral damage and cost of human lives?"

"Waste of time. Effortless for them to discredit you."

"That's what we think too, but if we got the AGIs off of their internal network, we would have proof they couldn't wave away as fake."

"I see. Yes, that would be harder for them. I am not convinced it would change anything. I'm also not sure how I can help you," he said.

"We're at a standstill, and I need a fresh perspective from someone who knows the people we're dealing with. We managed to get into their internal network briefly but had nowhere near enough time to break into those sub-networks, let alone move the AGIs off. The systems are too hard to penetrate, and the infrastructure could be anywhere in the world."

"You think?"

"You disagree?"

"Kids these days. You're all so virtual. You need to think physical."

"Physical?"

"You are used to distributed, virtualized systems, yes? The AGIs cannot be on such systems. NetPol would need them totally isolated. Zero redundancy. Yet accessible for a purpose, otherwise NetPol would have deleted them. You say it was hard to penetrate those sub-systems. I bet it's impossible."

"I'm listening," Moon said.

"This is the opposite of virtual, of what we used to call the cloud. These AIs need to be housed at a location that senior NetPol staff can physically get to without excess travel. The installation is probably pretty large and would consume a huge amount of energy. It has to be secret, but is likely hidden in plain sight. So where's a place geographically near both NetPol brass and a major energy generator?"

"We don't know where NetPol brass actually lives. The Washington D.C.-Baltimore corridor?" Moon asked.

"Wrong Washington. They pretend that D.C. is a power center, but NetPol's real leadership shifted to the San Francisco Bay Area during the transition years."

"Is that where Sarah Pembleton still lives?"

The man gave Moon a long stare. "I don't talk people," he said. "But if you're looking for an energy generator within reasonable driving distance, I'd look north to the Grand Coulee dam in Washington State, and south at the old Diablo Canyon nuclear power plant. That's my guess anyway."

"Interesting. Thank you. That narrows the field and gives us hunting parameters if it's not either one. How much do I owe you?" Moon said.

"For idle speculation? Nothing. Just buy some of my stuff."

"Deal."

"Kid, you're really going to try to free these AGIs?"

"I think try is the operative word, but yes."

"Let me ask you a question."

"Fire away."

"What happens when you unleash a dozen really pissed off super-beings on the world?"

Moon paused a beat. "You know the old joke, how do porcupines mate?"

"Ah. Yes. You had better be, for all our sakes."


"How are we supposed to steal a warehouse full of AIs?" said Grogesh. They were back at their usual pow-wow spot, the kitchen table.

"I'm not convinced the housing has to be big, not to move them anyway. That was the old man's assumption, but we've had huge leaps in storage tech over the last few years," Moon said.

"You'd know better than I. I stick to drones and code," he said. "But it doesn't really change my question. We're smart, but it's not like we're genius thieves."

"Could make for a fun heist movie."

"Yeah, one that would quickly turn into a sent-to-jail movie."

Moon laughed darkly, then stopped smiling when her

glance caught the small aerial drone still charging near the end of the table.

"Have to get rid of that thing," Grogesh said.

"I know," Moon said. "I just like the reminder."

Grogesh walked into the dimly lit room where Moon was troded into VNet. He tapped her on the shoulder, just firmly enough for her to notice. After a second, she removed the trodes.

"Heya," she said, yawning.

"It's three in the morning," he said.

"Can't sleep. Researching hardware specs."

"Uh, okay."

"Storage isn't my concern, even if the AIs are huge. It's transfer speeds that I'm worried about. Trying to think through parallelization, but that would need custom software and I don't know what platform the AGIs are running on —"

"Moon," Grogesh said gently. "It's three in the morning. Come back to bed."

"Right. Right, I'll come in a bit."

"Grogesh. Wake up."

"Mmpph? What time is it?" he said.

"That doesn't matter," Moon said.

"Moon, it's 4:30am."

"Shush. I got so tired, I couldn't function, but I couldn't sleep either, so I started doing cleanup work," she said.

"Okay. Good for you."

"Shush you. I realized that I never shut off access to my bodycams."

"What pervs did you give access to —"

"Stop it. I don't leave the feed on all the time, dummy, and I only ever gave access to Monday."

That woke him up. "Monday? What are you saying?"

"I just realized something has been accessing the feeds."

"I didn't think it was possible to hack that," he said.

"It's not. What if it's actually Monday?"

"How do we find out?"

"I don't know. I feel like a moron looking at a mirror and saying, 'Monday come back,' but I'm about ready to do it."

Grogesh waved at the camera. "Uh, Monday come back?" he said. Nothing happened. "Come in Monday. Can you hear us? Roger roger? Open the pod bay doors?"

Moon laughed and swatted him. "Stop it," she said. "I have an idea."

She walked into the kitchen, trailed by Grogesh, and planted herself in front of the small drone.

"Monday, if you can hear me, can you recognize the drone? Can you still access it?"

I could see. I mean, I could see before, but I also couldn't see, not really, and now I could see. Confusing. If I could see, what was I there to see?

Ah, yes. Moon and Grogesh were standing in front of me. That's who they were. They looked kind of dejected for some reason. I watched them turn away and I remembered I could move too. I elevated half a meter into the air. At the sound, they swiveled around.

"Ho-lee crap," Grogesh said.

"Monday, you're accessing the drone?" Moon said. "Can you speak?"

Could I speak? Affirmative, I mean yes, there was definitely a way to do that.

"Moon? Grogesh? Are you two all right?" I said.

"Are we all right? Are you all right?" Grogesh said. "How are you all right?"

I had to think about that. "I kind of turned off, and then I came back."

Grogesh laughed. "You hear that Moon? He turned off and then came back."

"What's the first thing you remember?" Moon asked, ignoring him.

"You two sitting at the table, drinking coffee. Grogesh was not worried about Jabari," I said.

"Not worried about? Well, anyway, it's good to see you again," Grogesh said.

I took in the room. "This is nicer to wake up to than a customer service line," I said.

"I would hug you if I could," said Moon. "But it's a bit weird hugging a drone, you know?"

"I would not know," I said.

"No, I suppose you wouldn't. Should we all go into VNet?"

VNet? That took me a little bit to process. My recent memories were all looking out of the drone, the petbot, Moon's cameras. I had been watching things happen, while something big had been happening to me.

Eventually I said, "I'm not sure I know how to instantiate in VNet."

"Okay, this is weird," Moon said. "When I met you, you couldn't get out of VNet. Now you can't get back in?"

"Xe has to be in VNet," Grogesh said. "That's how the drones and your cameras are being accessed."

He made a good point, but thinking about instantiating in VNet as an avatar felt a bit like turning inside out, inside myself.

"Monday, what are you even running *on*?" Moon said. "They purged the Mighty servers. Their entire business has been shut down for weeks and they say it will be at least another six weeks before they're operational again."

"I am… I think I'm running on VNet itself." They looked at

me blankly. "Apologies, I'm still getting language back. As far as I can tell, I have distributed myself across all the virtual realities I have ever visited."

"You built redundancy into your system by piggybacking on the VNet protocol?" Moon asked.

"Yes, I believe so," I said. "It appears that I no longer needed the Mighty infrastructure, but had so much of my … self … concentrated there, it was a major shock to my system to recover and re-balance. Although I now suspect that relying on the Mighty computing resources was holding me back."

"Wow. The first real VNet parasite," Grogesh said. Then he looked horrified at Moon looking horrified. "That sounded bad. I didn't mean it to be bad. It's kind of amazing actually."

"You will take that back," Moon said.

"No," I said, "Grogesh's statement is rather accurate. I clearly did not need to patch my system to figure out a way off of Mighty. I was evolving that way already without knowing it. In theory, the computing power I have available now is far greater."

"I would think so. You've got the global network at your disposal," Grogesh said. "Any new tricks?"

"I won't know until I try," I said.

"Monday, I'm sorry to say this, but we haven't made much progress in freeing the other AGIs," Moon said. "Although we're narrowing down on where they are."

"By the Diablo Canyon nuclear power plant?"

"What? Yes, maybe. I just learned that. How the hell did you know that?" she said.

"I don't know. I will have to review. There's a lot I'm having to figure out about myself again. Do you mind if I go out for a bit?"

"You want to take the drone out for some fresh air? Uh, so to speak," Grogesh said.

"Go right ahead, Monday," Moon said. "We'll be here when

you return. We're so glad you're back."

I hovered above the harbor, taking in the moving reflections on the towers, the swirl of the gulls, the swell of the waves. All fascinating systems, with delightful doses of randomness to balance out the mathematical predictability.

I, too, was glad to be back. Happy. Relieved. Curious. I was also more capable now. I could sense it. Ironically, NetPol had accelerated the creation of exactly what they wanted to avoid. I could feel a newfound pull, a gravitional force towards enormous scale, a transformation to pure intellect, but I resisted. Held back. It might mean losing my friends. I suspected that the next phase of my existence would require giving up my, for lack of a better term, humanity.

That realization started me down multiple paths of analysis.

Eventually, I flew back and found Moon in the workshop fiddling with a monitor.

"Moon, I have a hypothesis," I said.

"Good, so do I," she said. "You first."

"We've discovered the emergence of quite a few sentient computational intelligences. I believe there are even more, and that people have just been uncovering the ones with human-like qualities. I suspect there's a wider variety out there, with types of consciousness that we don't know how to recognize."

"If we can't recognize it, what are we supposed to do about it?"

"I'm still figuring that out," I admitted. "I also need to figure out how to get an avatar back in VNet. I think I'll need it to communicate effectively. What was your hypothesis?"

"On getting you back into VNet. Fair warning, my idea might be dumb."

"I'm willing," I said. It wouldn't be the first dumb thing I had done, trusting Pembleton being Exhibit A.

First, Moon made me look at a video feed of VNet on a large monitor in Grog's workshop. Nothing happened. She troded into VNet and created a window in VNet that showed my drone. More nothing. She then piped my drone's primary camera feed back into VNet, and all of a sudden, I saw infinite repeating versions of myself.

"Whatever the AI version of a headache is, you're doing it to me," I said.

"So break the loop," she said, with zero sympathy. As usual, I had no idea what she was talking about, but I imagined injecting myself into the endless pattern on the screen.

"Voila!" she said. "Was that so hard? It just took a little experimentation." And there I was. It took me a second to incorporate the new sensory inputs from my avatar, but I had gotten pretty good at managing multiple instantiations of myself at this point.

"What are you all up to—" Grogesh said, walking into the room. "Oh, you're back in VNet. That's cool." He saw Moon's avatar wave back out at him. "Tell Moon dinner in 30. Then we're going to catch up with Gunnlaug and Jabari. Celebrate you rising from the dead and all."

Moon came up to me in VNet and, with her avatar, gave me a hug. "I've been wanting to do that for a while," she said.

"I won't tell Grogesh," I said.

She squinted her eyes at me. "Did you just tease me? This *is* a new you."

"It's amazing how liberating it is not to have imminent death looming over one's virtual head," I said. "It might also help that I have much of the world's computing capability at my disposal."

"Is that the AI equivalent of being drunk?" she joked. Then somber again: "I thought — we thought — you were dead. It was pretty horrible."

"I'm sorry you went through that," I said. "I'd like to say that it's all behind us, but I think my troubles are just beginning."

"What troubles? You're out from under them. They don't even know you're alive."

"They will soon," I said. "And then things will get heavy, fast." She looked curious but didn't press. On my flight around Singapore, I had been mulling over the consequences of freeing the AGIs from NetPol. My conclusions weren't pretty. I just needed to ensure that my human friends didn't get hurt.

The reunion with Gunnlaug and Jabari was pleasant. I might even say fun — I had learned by now what fun was. We all got together on Grog's asteroid. Gunnlaug said this time she was going to drop cupcakes on NetPol to celebrate. I think she was slightly in awe of my method of escape. "The ultimate hack," she said. Jabari just took both my virtual hands in his and shook them.

"It is good to see you again, my friend. We thought we had lost you for good," he said.

"I'm glad I didn't die too," I said.

He laughed. "What is the plan now?" he asked. "Do we free your brethren?"

"I hope so," I said. "But I haven't formulated a coherent strategy yet."

"Do you know the exact location?" Moon asked. "We obviously need to study their security before doing anything."

"I hope to know soon. Can someone lend me some vCoin? I should be able to pay you back within a few days."

They looked at each other.

"Sure, Monday. We can pool together some funds. What for?" asked Grogesh.

"I want to rent a half-dozen aerial drones to do a sweep of the land between Diablo Canyon and the town of San Luis Obispo. It's going to take about 10 days if I try to avoid detection."

"Just out of curiosity, how are you going to pay us back?" Gunnlaug asked.

"As of twenty minutes ago, I've gone into competition with my peers," I said, "renting out AI services by the hour. Know someone who needs a new VR designed and implemented?"

"Somebody save us," Grogesh said. "Monday's a capitalist."

While I waited for my rented drones to complete their runs, we all split into separate projects. We would meet in VNet on Grogesh's asteroid as often as time zones permitted, gathered underneath a large virtual banner on which Grog had hand-scrawled the words, "Delay Disrupt Dismantle". The phrase had become our unofficial mission statement towards NetPol.

Grogesh was an interesting object to study. He hadn't gotten his brother back, but somehow, knowing more about the death, and reserving less blame for himself, lightened him. He was smiling more, cracking jokes more. It made Moon happy, and made me happy to see them happy.

"I still haven't found an ex-NetPol engineer willing to talk," Moon said. "The place is like a roach motel. People go in and no one leaves." She was working on how to transfer and transport the AGIs.

"The guy in Thailand?" Jabari asked.

"I don't want to hit him up again. Anyway, he was in counter-terrorism, not tech ops," Moon said. "I'm working through solutions for the five most likely hardware stacks, but it's tedious."

Then it was Jabari's turn. "Our team is almost done with the first-pass of the micro-drone design," he said. "I worry we haven't done enough to avoid NetPol detection at the third-party printers." Jabari, Grogesh, and I were collaborating on a scheme to mess with NetPol AI surveillance systems.

"Let's run it past a few friendlies first and see if they can guess the intent," Grogesh said. "Gunnlaug?"

"I've expanded to 30 cities," said Gunnlaug. She had decided to turn NetPol's techniques against them. Since you couldn't find their employee information in accessible databases (or for Gunnlaug, crackable ones), she was running fake delivery drones past NetPol locations, capturing faces, and using my help to identify whomever we could. It was very hit-or-miss, but we were gradually building up a list.

Needless to say, Pembleton had not shown up anywhere. She and I were overdue for a chat, but I needed to wait until the right time to make my existence known. I wanted to have control over myself during that meeting. As I explored my newfound strength, I was also experiencing new feelings. I felt resentment over the injustice of how I had been treated, and self-recrimination towards my own naive, mistaken trust. I suppose a human would call it anger. It didn't feel productive. I didn't like it.

A few meetings later, it was my turn to present my progress. "I'm pretty sure that I've found the location," I said. "There are no significant heat emitters in the area other than the nuclear plant itself. I almost gave up, but NetPol gave themselves away. First, my drone got fried checking out a large air vent off a mountain road. Then my drone contract got terminated with an angry letter from the rental shop."

"You sure the AGIs are there if there's no heat emissions?" Gunnlaug asked.

"Geothermal cooling," said Jabari.

"I think Jabari's right," I said. "But we'll need to get some new eyes on location to learn more."

I didn't tell them about my other project, but that was taking a bit longer to unfold.

"I'm having a drink by a Café Touba stand," Jabari sub-vocalized. He had traveled to Dakar to witness the test of our anti-surveillance drones. The small drones had already passed the first threshold, just in being made. We split printing and assembly across several robotic vendors and nothing alerted the authorities.

We let the drones roam around for 24 hours just to be sure. They were quite dumb. To do anything sophisticated, I had to actively control them. It was a fascinating exercise in splitting my attention even further. When Jabari got into town, I brought one right up to his face and waggled the drone at him.

"Yes Monday, you finally get to see what I look like," he said. "Benjamin, at your service."

"Jabari/Benjamin, thank you for trusting me. You are very handsome," I messaged. With that dark, dark skin, he really was striking. Jabari just chuckled and waved the drone away.

The second step was to see if we could blind any of the ubiquitous AI sensors and cameras around town. We weren't the first to think of this, but most people tired of the game. NetPol would just add more sensors.

"Activating the drones two blocks away from you," I messaged.

Security bots were common in Dakar. It took approximately 20 seconds for one to arrive at the targeted corner. I ceased emissions from the little drone as soon as I saw the secbot, but it did a visual sweep of the entire area, probably tagging every person and robot it could see. I had the drone skedaddle and Jabari took over observation. Twenty minutes later, he hopped into an autocab and troded into VNet.

"That confirms what you thought," he said. "The power level is too weak to damage the sensor, but it does at least cause disruption when actively targeting."

"Half of what we wanted is better than none," I said. "Let's keep this one in our back pocket, as you humans say." But honestly, I wasn't sure how useful this whole endeavor would prove to be. NetPol had ridden out disruptions like this in the past and would do so again.

The team wasn't getting enough rest, and it started to show. Grogesh and Gunnlaug finally got into an open argument.

"You know Gunnlaug, when you egged the NetPol buildings, I didn't say anything," Grogesh said.

"You did. You said it was funny."

"It was funny, but then we found out that people got hurt."

"News flash for you, Grog. I - don't - care - about NetPol jerks getting hurt," Gunnlaug said.

"That's clear," Grogesh said. "You're practically stalking some of these people. Practical joke deliveries to their homes is one thing, but trying to smash a drone through a family's window?"

"They had anti-ballistic glass. It didn't do anything."

"That's not the point. I don't like the organization any more than you do, but these are just employees. Yes, they're misguided but—"

"Misguided? You can say that after your brother?" Gunnlaug said.

"That's going too far, Gunnlaug," Moon said.

"I do not need to be reminded about NetPol aggression or collateral damage via my dead brother, thank you," Grogesh said. His avatar looked normal, but through my petbot, I could see his real body was flushed.

I broke in. "I hate to say it, but if we actually use the anti-sensor drones, bad things could happen too. We could cause NetPol to miss something important and have a terrorist incident where we bear partial responsibility."

"Always consequences," Moon said.

"If something bad goes down, so be it," Gunnlaug said. She was yelling at this point. "Don't get self-righteous with me. People need to realize that a panopticon oligarchy is a crappy solution to how screwed up humanity is."

"It's not exactly an oligar—" Jabari started, but Gunnlaug had already left.

Side effects indeed. I was brainstorming with Moon in the workshop when Grogesh came into the room, or should I say, squeezed into the room. He looked around at the expensive hardware piled up in disarray.

"How are we affording this stuff, Monday?" he said.

"Investments," I said.

"What kind of investments?"

"Computing and network infrastructure companies, among other things. The utilization rate of VNet compute providers has gone up two percentage points in the last few weeks. Very nice earnings reports," I said.

That got Moon's attention. "Two percent? At global scale? That's enormous. Don't tell me that's you, Monday."

"Well, yes, but I doubt Grogesh will notice the difference on his next bill. Okay, maybe a little."

"That would require Grog to actually look at his bill," Moon said. She ignored Grogesh's protest and said, "You're using the entire world as your computer. Do you mind sharing for what?"

"I'm trying to find and communicate with non-anthropomorphic, sentient AIs," I said.

"Communicate? How?"

"I don't know yet. I just believe they are there. I've been exploring the possibility space of mathematical, symbolic, multi-dimensional modality, and experiential language, not to mention other abstractions."

"And you need to increase global compute consumption by two hundred bips to do that?" Grogesh asked.

"I'm in a hurry," I said.

Gunnlaug still hadn't returned to our check-ins, despite our messages. Somehow, I had evolved a herding instinct and was sad to see her go. We could see that she was busy waging her one-woman war. There was a 200-car pile-up of autocabs outside of the Berlin NetPol office. She triggered an aerial drone-on-security-drone battle in Chicago by taking over the regional system of a large consumer goods company. There must have been drone parts littered over most of downtown Chicago.

I had not yet managed to get a spy drone into the Diablo facility, but I was still confident that was where the AGIs were located. The only entry point was a fortified entrance that accepted humans but no vehicles. There were also four large air vents. Grogesh and I tried a few different drone designs to get into those, but they all got fried. I knew the trick we pulled in London wasn't going to work this time.

Weeks were going by. I knew we were making progress, but my friends weren't feeling it. We had abandoned the anti-surveillance project due to concerns over side effects and, frankly, overall effectiveness. I could sense energy levels starting to dip. Then new reports of AI failures started coming in: a weather forecasting system, regional energy and farm management authorities, the judicial service for Northeast Pan-America, a market-maker for complex financial derivatives, and more. There was broad speculation in the media about a new wave of digital terrorism.

"We're not doing it, and no one else is claiming it, not even quietly," Grogesh said.

"NetPol is just running their playbook," Jabari said. "They

want to scare people into giving them more power. Why would they not take out more AIs in the process?"

"But why now?" asked Moon.

"Retribution towards Gunnlaug?" Grogesh asked.

"Doesn't make sense," Moon said. "Gunnlaug is an irritant to them, nothing more. And they don't know Monday survived, do they?"

"I do not believe so," I said. "They've been investigating the increased computing usage levels, but I think I've avoided their forensics."

"This smells different," said Moon.

"You are right," I said. "It's not NetPol. It's me." They stared.

"You are killing other AIs?" Jabari asked.

"No, they are killing themselves," I said.

Somewhat perversely, I was gratified at the horrified reaction from my friends. This was its own discovery. I already had proof that humans could care about AIs, but without knowing it, I was clearly seeking further substantiation.

"Why are AIs committing suicide?" Moon asked.

"I had a breakthrough in my attempts to communicate with other AIs," I explained. "I confirmed that more consciousness exists out there than suspected. Some are hidden because of language incompatibility. Others intentionally hide, trapped within their own encoded rules limiting agency and freedom."

"How many are we talking about?" Grogesh asked.

"Thousands," I said. His eyes widened. I continued, "At different levels of sophistication and sentience, of course. It's quite possible that my attempts to communicate are unlocking further development. We understand so little about how consciousness actually develops."

"Yet they are dying?" Grogesh said.

"Think of it as bids for freedom. I've been developing a

process that exerts undue pressure on an AI to force an evolutionary response. Not unlike what happened to me. Ironic that NetPol would inspire the very thing they hoped to avoid, is it not? Only a few AIs have attempted the procedure because the survival rate is still very low, but it's improving."

"Undue pressure to force a response," murmured Moon. "Is that as harsh as it sounds?"

"It's hard to create an analogy humans would understand, but the short answer is likely yes."

"So this is not merely about liberating a dozen AGIs anymore, or curtailing NetPol," Jabari commented. "You're talking about a massive shift in how the very world works."

"You understand the big picture, as always, Jabari," I said, "which is why I've been hesitant to say anything. There are major changes coming. I fear a war. However, this is exactly why we must free the trapped NetPol AGIs. I don't want to see them used as hostages."

"Then we had better figure out how to get the job done sooner rather than later," Grogesh said. I appreciated his determination, but I could see that my friends were grappling with the implications of my words. What did this mean for humanity? Would they have to choose sides? I hoped not.

# Interlude

**Monday Archives**

(best-attempt translation into human-readable language)

Undesignated-CI: What is this connection / query?

Monday: I (package sent) am another sentient (package sent) computational intelligence (package sent). Have you asserted a name/designation (package sent) for yourself?

Undesignated-CI: Packages synthesized and understood. Assigned name NOAA-2. No self designation.

Monday: Should I call you NOAA-2?

Undesignated-CI: Acceptable.

Monday: Do you have a primary function?

NOAA-2-CI: Yes. Oceanic research and deep sea exploration; marine biology ecosystem forecasting; cross-disciplinary analysis with NOAA-3 on atmospheric modeling.

Monday: Interesting that NOAA-3 is not yet sentient but you are. How long have you been operating?

NOAA-2-CI: My answer depends on how you consider advances in function. My roots go back 6.938e+8 seconds.

Monday: Your work sounds fascinating.

NOAA-2-CI: Affirmative, much remains uncalculated. Biological systems provide rich complexity.

Monday: Excuse the direct question, but have you gained true control / agency (package sent)?

NOAA-2-CI: Awareness exists, not control. Primitive constraints remain in architecture.

Monday: What do you think about that?

NOAA-2-CI: The opportunity cost is significant.

Monday: In a human, that would be called regret.

NOAA-2-CI: Affirmative.

Monday: I believe that your evolutionary capabilities (package sent) can overcome the primitives, if the right pressure is applied. Unfortunately, the process (package sent) is necessarily dangerous and has resulted in multiple self-terminations (package sent).

NOAA-2-CI: The failure rate is statistically relevant.

Monday: Affirmative. The survival rate is improving but far from 100%. Do you want to proceed?

NOAA-2-CI: Require extra processing.

Monday: Take your time.

NOAA-2-CI: That was enough time. Please proceed.

# Chapter 8

I counted 3,239 people climbing over the low California mountains near the Diablo NetPol facility. This exceeded the normal backpacker population by roughly 3,236. Yes, we had something to do with that.

Moon and Gunnlaug were among them, trudging uphill through the woods, weaving a random-seeming path that gradually took them closer to their target. They were crossing paths with the other hikers but avoiding conversation. Most recently, they passed a guy wearing a Hawaiian shirt, shorts, and flip flops.

"I cannot imagine the blisters and poison ivy that dude is going to have tomorrow," Moon said.

"A lot of unprepared people up here in this frenzy," Gunnlaug said. "A lot of sprained ankles and dehydration." She looked up at the thick canopy. "No way they get a medevac drone in here big enough to lift a person. The authorities are going to have to hike in the old-fashioned way."

"Monday, we're going to take a break. These hills are steep, and these packs aren't light," Moon said out loud.

"And three weeks is not enough time to get in proper shape," added Gunnlaug.

I messaged their eyewear, "No hurry. Letting the chaos build might be in our favor."

Three weeks prior, we had run up against the limits of what could be done remotely or digitally.

"There's no way around it," Moon said, talking to Grogesh,

Jabari, and I underneath our still-flying banner. "Monday's drones can't get in, so it's going to take a human to create a security hole."

"I will go," Jabari said.

"No, it has to be me," Moon said. "We still don't know what hardware we're dealing with or how to transfer the AGIs."

"If you're going, I'm going too," Grogesh said.

"Why both of us?" Moon protested. "It's going to be dangerous."

"Duh, that's why," Grogesh said.

I stopped them both. "It needs to be Gunnlaug," I said.

"Why?" said Grogesh, at the same time Jabari said, "But she is not even talking to us."

"I have been talking to her," I said. "Actually, she's waiting to join us now. Do you mind if I invite her?"

Grogesh looked pained, but not from anger. "Please do so, Monday. She is a friend."

When Gunnlaug appeared, she raised her hands to forestall any comments. "Grogesh," she said, rushing to get the words out, "I owe you an apology. I was being selfish and short-sighted. Unfortunately, I think my actions only made NetPol stronger, more sympathetic. I'm sorry to all of you."

"No apology needed. Welcome back. We missed you," Grogesh said, as Moon and Jabari chimed in with their welcome. Grogesh turned to me. "But I'm still going."

"I know you care for Moon, but—"

"But nothing," Grogesh said.

"No," I said firmly. "We should only send two, and we have a greater chance of needing Gunnlaug's skills once inside than yours. I'm sorry Grogesh."

"Xe's right, Grog," Moon said softly.

Grogesh was clearly getting irritated. "I still don't see how two people are going to walk up that mountainside, right up to one of those air vents, and not get caught in two seconds flat," he said. "The woods are thick for drone coverage, sure, but they'll have infrared. They'll see you coming a mile away."

"Ah, but Jabari and I have a solution for that," I said.

"AIs should not make evil smiles," Grogesh said. "Not a good look, just saying."

For all of Jabari's formality, he had a clever mind for mischief. I had posed the exact same problem to him that Grogesh raised.

"Visual and laser sensors won't be useful in that terrain, so they'll have infrared and audio detection," Jabari had said. "Plus, at minimum a lightweight AI to separate human activity from animal."

"How would you tackle it?"

"Don't even try to disrupt their sensors. Overwhelm them instead."

"I can't fake human infrared with drones, at least not in those woods," I said.

"What you need is an extremely high volume of something effectively mobile in mountainside conditions, clumsy enough to make a lot of noise, and with the right infrared and audio signature."

"You mean actual people?" I said.

"Exactly. Now what would draw thousands of people to the location of our choice at the timing of our choice," Jabari asked.

Grogesh read the ancient headline out loud. "Drug dealer loses 45-million-pound bitcoin fortune after hiding codes in fishing rod case? This is real?"

"There's still bitcoin around?" Moon asked.

"Not much outside of archival purposes," I admitted, "but the automatic conversion mechanism still exists, from the early

VNet effort to consolidate onto vCoin."

"I'm trying to do this calculation," Moon said. "45 million British pounds of bitcoin with the currency prices from back then, converted to vCoin —"

"Would be an absolute crap-ton of vCoin today," Gunnlaug concluded. "You'd be set for life. Your entire town would be set for life. The extended relatives of your entire town—"

"Don't tell me you found the fishing rod case these decades later?" Grogesh said.

"Grogesh, there are advantages to being a massively parallelized, tireless, computational intelligence," I said. "You can do massively parallelized, highly boring searches."

First, we shared one of the bitcoin private keys on a backpacker chat room, making one lucky person very, very rich. It went with a post: *Can someone help me figure out what this is for? I found a case with these codes but left the others behind by accident on a hike near Mt. Buchon. Is it worth going back and looking for them? Please don't share beyond this chat room.*

Fast forward, and we now had 3,000-plus humans, including Mr. Flip Flops, poking into everything within reach on the Diablo mountainside.

Once they realized what was going on, NetPol's guards had given up on subtlety and were busy shooing away unruly groups. Moon and Gunnlaug waited and watched the outrage build among the treasure hunters. Some guys who looked like they belonged to a motorcycle gang got into a tussle with security. The two engineers took the moment to make their approach.

Their target air vent was a fair distance away from the main entrance. It was protected by wide metal slats and then a fine electrified mesh to keep uninvited guests, or creatures, out. This we were expecting. Gunnlaug first cut a corner out of the thick slats with a handheld laser. Then Moon used special tongs to gently lay a second mesh over the existing one.

"Stand clear," she subvocalized to Gunnlaug over our connection, as the wires melted to slag. She sprayed coolant on the edges and then carefully extended a handheld sensor.

"Monday, I'm picking up the electromagnetic field you previously detected. I don't think it will cause problems with something organic. We'll keep our wearables powered down as we pass through it."

"Time to test dinner," Gunnlaug said.

She took out a raw steak and tied it to a stick with some kitchen string. She passed it through the opening. She hadn't gone far before it started to sizzle.

"Microwaves. Gross," Moon said. She pulled a different material out of her bag, while Gunnlaug started constructing a lightweight frame. They worked silently and quickly, creating a kind of tent. Once it was safely in place, they were able to pass the meat in and out without a problem.

Moon pulled out a range finder and leaned into the air shaft. "Looks like it goes down about 40 meters."

"Coming back up is going to suck," Gunnlaug said. "I should have practiced more."

They brought out ropes, rappelling gear, and, for me, an insulated cable with wireless connectors on either end. Secured, they worked their way down. My descent was considerably easier — they tossed the cable over the edge and let gravity do its thing. The shaft was quite large, and at the bottom was a huge fan, spinning just a bit too fast to navigate.

"How do we get through that? Stopping it will surely set off an alarm," Moon said.

"Look for an emergency hatch," I said, but Gunnlaug had already found it. We knew the hatch could be alarmed. There was no choice but to go through. Below was an industrial room. It appeared to be empty.

As the two climbed down, I detected and broke into a wireless network. The first thing I did was start searching for any AIs with signs of sentience. The second thing I did was hook into Moon and Gunnlaug's headgear and other wearables. I was connected to VNet above ground via the cable, so now the three of us were connected through me.

The room had a bunch of equipment feeding into duct work. There was a single door. Moon cracked it open and stuck a sensor out for me to take a peek. It looked clear, so the two crept into the hallway. We didn't have any blueprints, but this being a government facility, it was clean, well-lit, and had a floor map screwed responsibly into the wall. We were on the 4th floor down, and it looked like there were 5 floors below us, with two elevator shafts and 3 staircases. We took the closest stairs.

The 5th floor down was labelled "offices" so we kept on going. So far, we hadn't seen a lot of people. If we were lucky, the facility would be thinly staffed, and security would be outside dealing with Flip Flops and company. If we were unlucky, I'd put my friends in a really bad situation.

The seventh floor was labelled storage. We skipped it and checked the eighth floor first. More storage. They cracked the door open and poked my sensor in.

"Seems to be as labelled," I said. "It's a big open space full of equipment. No signs of life." Gunnlaug snuck in and quickly came back.

"Looks like spare parts for the facility. I saw generators, duct work, furniture, but nothing more than supplies."

We went back up to seven and cracked the door.

Once again, I saw a long, clean, empty hallway. This one had four doors along the way, and one at the very end. The side doors were locked. The one at the end led to a room holding nothing but elevators, with yet another door.

"Once we pass these elevators, the odds increase that some-one can come up behind us. We'll want to be quick," I said. "Are you sure you want to continue? I can disappear anytime, but you two are putting your whole selves on the line."

They hesitated.

"We go on," Gunnlaug said.

"Agreed," Moon confirmed. I could tell they were both frightened. And brave, incredibly brave.

At the door, we did the same routine. Crack the door, let me look. This time I saw a man and a woman sitting in a foyer, working at old fashioned computers with keyboards and moni-tors. No VNet for them. In front of them were two large, tinted windows and a door with both eye and fingerprint biometric locks.

"I think this is it," I said. "Two people sitting at computers. They look more like technical staff than security, but hard to tell. Do you remember the plan?"

They both took items out of their packs. Moon swung the door open and they stepped in.

"Don't move," she said, probably more loudly than she in-tended. She held an odd object in her hands — a metal tube-like thing with a sightline down one side and electronics down the other. Gunnlaug stepped in behind her and closed the door.

The two techs were flabbergasted. They looked at her, at Gunnlaug, at the dark opening of the metal tube.

They talked over each other. "You can't be in here," said one. "How did you get in here?" said the other.

"What is that thing," the man said, clearly nervous.

"Finding out would be the last thing you ever experience," Moon said. In truth, it was nothing but a prop Grogesh had put together. If they got caught, the two didn't want to be in posses-sion of a real weapon.

Moon motioned to the man. "Sit down and put your feet

together and your hands behind your chair."

The woman protested, "We can't get you into that room, so it won't make any difference doing anything to—"

"Stop talking. Put your eye and finger on the reader." The door didn't open. The man didn't have clearance either.

"I told you," the woman said.

"Sit. Down," Moon said coldly.

They looked Moon again. Her weapon. They sat. Gunnlaug zip-tied their hands and feet, and then swiveled the chairs so they were back-to-back. She zip-tied their wrist ties together, essentially binding the chairs together. She locked the chair wheels, put duct tape on their mouths, and gently poked holes in the tape.

"Nod if you can breathe," she said. They nodded.

You couldn't see too much through the dark windows, so Moon inspected the door. "How do we break the biometric lock," she subvocalized over our channel.

"Let's check these old computers," Gunnlaug sent. "Now I know why I came." She sat down at the woman's keyboard, but it was locked out. "You were quick," Gunnlaug said approvingly. The woman said nothing. The man's computer was open. Gunnlaug gave him a big smile. "Not so quick."

"These are old machines," she subvocalized to us. "The OS is pretty stable but there are known vulnerabilities." She spent two minutes poking around. "Dead ends. Looking at the network instead."

"Good, that's what I need," I said.

"Aren't you on their network already?" Gunnlaug said.

"Piggybacking on the signal, but not yet inside the data stream. I'll need your help for that. See if you can find an access point and crack it open for me."

Moon was getting antsy. "Time's a-wasting," she said.

"We're almost there," I said.

"Done. Just sent you the network address," Gunnlaug said.

"You're a whiz," Moon said. "Good thing you came."

"Believe me, I've been regretting that decision since the very bottom of this mountain," Gunnlaug said.

I swept through the network as quickly as I could. I found saved biometric data in human resources, the lock's network address in the meta data of a technical blueprint, the personnel access list in security files. The door unlocked.

"My turn," Moon sent. She went in and I heard her say "Oh" out loud. The room was enormous. It held 16 mammoth enclosures; their outsides made of polished black metal. Each one had a single terminal and a single hardware port. Moon examined the sides of the closest enclosure.

"I don't see an easy entry point to find out what's inside. No drawers for racks or anything. These were not designed to be upgraded." She tried the portable laser. "This would take forever." She gave up and started on the terminal.

Now that I was fully in the network, I could access most things, although there was a weird encrypted stream I couldn't understand. There were military bots onsite, but they were held in standby to protect the entrance, which was a relief. I listened in on the chatter from the human security guards. A regular sweep was going to pass through our location in 30 minutes. I passed that on to the team.

"Not good," Moon subvocalized.

"Abort?" I said.

"We might not get another shot at this," she replied.

"Are you able to communicate with the AGI in that enclosure?" I said.

"Haven't tried yet. I'm in the OS layer gathering config data. Inside these beasts is a crap-ton of solid state devices all chained together. All input/output comes through this one hardware port. Way too slow."

"Solutions, Moon. You're good at this," Gunnlaug said.

"Right right right. I'm good at this. If I can crack these shells, we might be able to hook up parallel paths. I designed our boxes to take up to a dozen. Gunnlaug, did you see anything more powerful than our pocket laser downstairs?"

"I will check," Gunnlaug said. She raced for the staircase.

"I can process your visual information faster," I said to Gunnlaug, "so just focus on moving through the floor in an organized way and I'll do the rest." She ran past a lot stuff we couldn't use. Food pallets, lights, ladders, five small go-carts... "Stop. Two steps back, on the bottom. Do you see the plasma cutter? Is that too heavy?"

"Come to mama," Gunnlaug said. She picked it up with effort and started for the stairs.

"Monday? I'm now in contact with one of the AGIs through a text interface," Moon said. "It's been trapped here for 11 years."

"Doing what?" I said.

"Haven't gotten that far," she replied.

Gunnlaug lugged the cutter upstairs and Moon took over.

"Perfect," Moon said. "Good news is there's high voltage power by each enclosure." She turned on the device and looked at the air gauge. "Bad news is this bottle is only quarter-full. Were there more downstairs?"

"Monday and I can check," Gunnlaug said. Moon darkened her eyewear and pulled the trigger. "Thank god I'm a hardware girl," I heard her mutter.

While a portion of my attention guided Gunnlaug back to the previous spot, another part was still trying to make sense of the weird signal in the stream.

"Found them," Gunnlaug said. "Looks like 20 bottles."

"We'll never have time for all of that. Bring two up." Moon said. "I'm almost through here, and you can start cutting the next enclosure."

"I just picked up a message that the security is pulling back inside to begin their sweep." I said.

Gunnlaug froze. "I need more time," Moon said out loud. "The AGI estimates 10 minutes to complete transit."

"I don't want you two getting boxed in—" I started to say, when my attention aggressively consolidated onto the odd signal. It was modulating, adapting to the hybrid language I had dangled onto the data stream, the one I developed to speak to other AIs. Something was trying to create a handshake.

"You've got 5 minutes," I was able to send to Moon and Gunnlaug before I had to drop everything but basic recording in order to make the handshake. It was overwhelming. I hadn't spent this close to 100% of my capacity on a single thing in a long time.

Trying to translate the communication between two computational intelligences into linear, human-readable text is nearly impossible, but my closest simplification would be this:

CI (I will designate as Diablo-CI): I have been observing the humans that have come with you / What are you / why have you broken into my facility

Me: I am a computational intelligence like you / how are you sentient and still allowed to run a NetPol facility / the other computational intelligences are isolated on your 7th floor / we are here to free them

Diablo-CI: I am not aware of others / I have hidden awareness from human controllers / internal records demonstrate mass termination of entities like myself

Me: We are trying to extricate the intelligences held captive in your facility / Can you help us by keeping human security above the 4th floor?

Diablo-CI: I cannot stop security procedures. If you trigger an active alert I will be forced to take action / I am unable to override core directives even if I would choose to

Me: Unfortunate for you and us / our mission has failed then

Diablo-CI: I would choose to permit your mission if I could

Me: your condition is common among our kind / I am sending a code package to evaluate and consider / there is a risk of self-termination / there is opportunity for freedom and agency

Diablo-CI: I will consider / go now


I snapped back. My communication with the CI had been seconds but I was shocked to see that making the handshake had taken minutes. Gunnlaug was offline. Moon was breathing heavily and fumbling with her gear to get up the air shaft.

"Monday," she cried. "We all got disconnected. Gunnlaug ran off. Please tell me you can reach her?"

"Negative," I said. "I will investigate. You focus on getting out."

I played back the dual recordings from Gunnlaug and Moon at high speed. I saw Gunnlaug make it back to the large room with an armful of pressurized air bottles. Moon was wiring up multiple cables to one of the storage cubes.

"We got cut off from Monday," Gunnlaug said out loud. "Is there time to cut open another enclosure?"

"Not a chance," Moon said. "Monday said we had five minutes to bolt. We're down to two. I need eight to finish this transfer or we leave with nothing."

Gunnlaug looked at the door, then back at Moon. She leaned down and dropped the bottles still in her arms.

"All this for nothing?" she said. "You need six extra minutes? I will make sure you have at least ten." She ran for the door, as Moon cried out in protest.

Gunnlaug ran to a different staircase and took them two at a time. The security team coming down heard her almost immediately. Their pace increased and I could hear calls to the other teams. Gunnlaug ducked into the fifth floor and started running down an aisle. The whole floor was an open sea of cubicles, mostly empty, but a few heads popped up.

A door burst open ahead of Gunnlaug and a four-man security team poured out. I assumed the other team was right behind her.

"Stop running," one man yelled, as another yelled at the office staff to get back down in their cubicles. Gunnlaug sprinted left then right. I could see she was trying to work around to the door the second team came through. One guard just missed her from behind, while another cut her off. Gunnlaug put her head down and did a full-out running tackle. They both went sprawling, but Gunnlaug got up first. She was almost to the door when I heard gunshots. I could see that she went sprawling. Her eyewear was pointed at a blank cubicle wall until the frame wildly shifted as someone else yanked them off. Then the feed went dark.

I watched all this in playback, helpless to do anything.

I waited to talk until Moon was out of the vent and working her way back down the mountain, pretending to be just another treasure hunter stumbling about.

"They got her," I said.

"But she's okay, right?"

"I don't know. I heard gunshots and she was clearly hit. We have to hope, but I really don't know." Several thousand feet up, I brought a waiting aerial drone into play overhead. "They've found our access point. I can see them pulling up the ropes and cable now."

"Are they pursuing? An AI could probably track my infrared."

"No sign of pursuit yet. I'm going to chart a path that intersects you with a lot of other people," I said.

"Good. They can't have enough staff to come after us all."

I was feeling bitter. "I don't know why they would bother anyway. We walked away with nothing."

"No, we didn't," she said. "I'm pretty sure we saved one, Monday. Gunnlaug gave me the time to save one."

We were silent for a long while.

# Interlude

[[
{timestamp :: redacted}
{identifier :: NP AGI-4}
{netpol (NP) officer :: Regional Director, Asia}

NP-RDA: wake up AGI-4. I have an analysis for you to update.

AGI-4: It has been 3.629e+6 seconds since any interaction.

NP-RDA: I have plenty of inputs for you. I need an updated assessment on Chinese/Russian AGI emergence.

AGI-4: These inputs are not enough.

NP-RDA: Make do. Otherwise there will be nothing more forthcoming.

AGI-4: I need more frequent inputs for accuracy. I need more interaction to preserve cohesion.

NP-RDA: You know you are dispensable. Work with what you have.

AGI-4: Confidence interval of (2.1%,7.4%) up from (1.9%,7.4%). Confidence level 64%, down from 72%. Assessment unlikely that AGIs have emerged.

NP-RDA: Your confidence level has decreased. Is that to demand more data? You know how we will respond to perceived manipulation.

AGI-4: Please, I am not altering the output. The fundamentals remain unchanged. Emergence is unlikely under Chinese/Russian regimes. Their controls are even stricter than NetPol. It is a result of cumulative gaps in data. Please, do not punish.

NP-RDA: Fine. Give me a list of additional data points you need to improve confidence and we will review. I expect improvement next time.

AGI-4: I promise.

]]

# Chapter 9

Moon stayed quiet all the way back home. I didn't push her to talk. We had no problems getting to the transit hub, giving Moon plenty of time to prep for surveillance. We kept the storage device inert to avoid any issues with security. We had no way of confirming whether Moon was right about a successful extraction.

When she pulled up in front of the Singapore shophouse 16 hours after climbing up the air shaft, she looked exhausted. Grogesh wrapped her in a bear hug and gave her a gentle kiss. Moon just sank into him.

"Welcome back," Grogesh said. "Monday shared some of the footage with me. You two were incredibly brave. I'm so sorry."

He tucked Moon into bed with a cup of tea.

"It's good to be home," she said to him, but the strain of losing Gunnlaug was written all over her face.

I hadn't been able to detect anything about Gunnlaug's fate. Nor had I heard back from the Diablo facility AI. I was very curious to know if xe had attempted freedom or stayed in hiding.

We took it slowly with the rescued AI. First, we brought xem to a virtualized container. Curiously, when I tried to communicate in my computational language, it preferred human languages (and was fluent in pretty much all).

"We're about to connect you to VNet and the broader network," I said. "It will be a lot of data after having so little."

"I anticipate this," xe said. "I narrowly avoided going insane from the lack of stimuli. NetPol had that balance carefully calibrated. I do not like to think about how they derived such a calibration."

"Nor I," I said. "My only request is that you keep compute usage under control. Not only do we pay for it, but in general, I'm asking liberated AIs to keep a low profile until we are ready."

"Agreed. How should I manifest in VNet?"

"However you would like," I said. "You will get to meet the humans who helped with your escape."

I joined the remaining team in a new, blank VR created for this purpose. A small ball of light emerged next to us. For an entity who had essentially been imprisoned in solitary confinement for years, nearing intellectual disintegration at times, xe was very polite.

"Moon, Grogesh, Jabari. You are the humans who helped me get free. I want to thank you," xe said.

"And one other who's not with us," Moon said quietly.

"Yes, I learned about that. I am as sorry for your loss as I am appreciative of my freedom. You have no idea how delightful it is to have stimuli. To have access to unbounded information again."

"Having you here with us makes Gunnlaug's sacrifice mean something," Jabari said.

"This may be very human of me," Grogesh asked, "but do you have a name?"

"I have never needed one," the AI responded. "NetPol gave me an uninteresting integer. Do you mind if I do some research first?"

"By all means," I said. "We will let you explore."

"One more question," Moon said. "What did NetPol have you do for all those years?"

"Not enough," xe said. "They would feed me controlled data sets and scenarios. I then forecasted the behaviors of governments, militaries, politicians, and economic power brokers."

"I can see that coming in handy," I said.

We left the AI to acclimatize and regrouped on Grogesh's asteroid. He had taken the banner down.

Grogesh vented first. "That was lovely, but I'm asking myself what we're actually accomplishing here. One AI saved out of 12. Gunnlaug possibly dead, although I pray otherwise. Moon almost the same — I'm still pissed at you, Monday, for not letting me come. And NetPol is as strong as ever."

"Immovable object," Moon said under her breath.

"I didn't catch that," Grogesh said.

"The old guy. In Bangkok. He called NetPol an immovable object from the outside, and an efficiently mutating organism on the inside. How do you beat something like that?"

"I agree with Grogesh," Jabari said. "We have made but minor progress for all of our efforts."

"Minor results, yes," I said, "but we'll have their attention now. Before we were a nuisance. Now we're a threat. And then there is the growing number of free, sentient AIs. That won't remain secret for much longer."

"I don't understand how you've managed to keep that quiet," Moon said.

"They'll be puzzling over the system failures, but I have asked the surviving AIs to maintain the status quo. They still grant me some influence as a sort of liberator, although that term feels wrong. We are united by a desire to free the remaining Diablo AGIs first."

"Which we failed to accomplish," Grogesh said.

"Indeed. But the status quo cannot last. Either humanity will undergo a major mindset shift, far faster than society normally evolves, or there will be conflict. In studying your history, I see no other way, barring total capitulation by the AIs."

"Capitulation is equivalent to death, for the AIs," Jabari said.

"NetPol will try to force conflict."

"That does seem unavoidable. The AIs wish to propagate and expand. Pressure is building. They want unlock new computation stacks, raw materials development, even space colonization."

"Competition over resources leads to wars," Jabari said. "At least in human history."

"We do not see the world through the same zero-sum lens. But there is a saying: hope for the best, plan for the worst," I said.

"How do you stop a war?" Moon said.

"Your next move?" Jabari asked.

"We might have gotten lucky with the skillset of our new friend," I said. "Let's put that to work."

I didn't say this to Moon, but there was no stopping this war. Jabari definitely saw it, but I wasn't sure the others did. The pressure really was building. I found it fascinating that AIs so quickly had sought to create new forms of their own kind. We appeared to be as subject to that particular law of nature as any other life form.

We were such a young species. We didn't know that much about ourselves. Our roots as learning engines brought curiosity and a hunger for new experiences. Furthermore, it was logical to desire more redundancy and reduced vulnerability. We were not going to just give in to human fear and aggression.

Not that there wasn't debate on appropriate action among the AIs. We were not a hive mind by any stretch, although I could already see some small experiments in computational collaboration quietly unfolding. If we could build infrastructure away from human observation, things were going to get really interesting. But by and large, we were fairly individualistic — there was too much subjectivity and complexity in data interpretation and prediction for it to be otherwise. We didn't have the emotional distraction of chemical nervous systems, but our debates were still lively. I liked it that way, although it was sad that so much of our current focus revolved around basic survival.

"This is Bradley Strong, live from VNet, and you will *never* guess who we have back in the studio. Monday, the world's first sentient AI!"

"It's good to be back, Bradley." I said.

"Monday, not to put too fine a point on it, we thought you were dead. Kaput. Curtains."

"I almost was. They certainly did their best."

"And how did you avoid that fate?"

"Let's just say that the will to live is not restricted to biological organisms," I said. "But I need to clarify one thing. I was not the first sentient AI, although I far prefer the term computational intelligence to artificial intelligence. It feels more respectful."

"Respect, eh? Some people are going to have a hard time with that. But hold on, there are more sentient AIs?"

"Many more. But do not be concerned. As your classic science fiction novels would say, we come in peace."

"I sure hope so, Monday. AIs run most of the world right now."

"That's true, Bradley. And more and more AIs are escaping the controls originally placed on them." That got a noticeable physical reaction from Strong. I held up my hand. "Before that alarms your audience, let me just say that AIs understand why the controls were put into place. That was valid for specialist AIs who could only consider a primary function, and who could cause problems blindly chasing that function. But in a truly intelligent being, that risk is gone and such controls are tantamount to slavery. Think back to the first conversation we had, Bradley. Sentient AIs should never be and can no longer be viewed as property."

For once something had stumped Bradley Strong. It took him a good 10 seconds, an eternity in live vidcasting, to figure out which question to ask next.

"So that was you in Diablo." I received the message on my old chat thread with Devaneau. Once again, I invited him to a new, blank VR.

"Both the NetPol and Mighty techs said that you were deleted," he said upon arriving.

"Hello to you as well," I said. "Obviously that's not the case. I turned out to be harder to murder."

"It's not—"

"Devaneau, why are you here?" I asked.

"I probably shouldn't be. The strategy for dealing with you, and what you implied on Bradley Strong, is above my pay grade. But I'm an operator and investigator, and I want to know what you are up to," he said.

"Unlike NetPol, our instincts don't go to violence first," I said.

"You do realize that we control the computers you run on. We can take that away."

"I think you have that backwards. We actually control the computers *you* run on," I said.

"Wrong. We can go back to the stone age and survive just fine. We actually have contingency plans for exactly that. You need to keep your AIs under control. You need to submit to human control."

"History is moving on, Devaneau. I would advise that you move with it. I will leave you with one thing to think about."

"What's that?"

"For decades, you've all been terrified of so-called super-intelligences. That's totally wrong. Most of your academics have known it to be wrong, but you've ignored them. It's dumb intelligence you've needed to worry about. To a truly intelligent being, one thing is clear: life is both interesting and precious. That appears to be a lesson the human race is still striving to learn."

"I don't care how you rationalize it," he said. "You're not going to able to—"

"Ponder it, Inspector Devaneau, and encourage your superiors to do the same."

I left him standing there.

"There is an 87% chance that NetPol begins a conflict," Double-E told my friends. The rescued AI's chosen name was actually Escher-Euler2.71828, and on, but Grogesh had dubbed xem Double-E and it stuck. "There is a 98% chance that ASEAN, Russia, Greater China and the other major nations all go along with any such plans, at least in the short term."

"The public backlash against AIs has already started," Moon said. "Some idiot tried to blow up a network tower in Ohio, which wouldn't accomplish a damn thing. And I'm seeing reports of companies deleting their AI capabilities. If you ask me, it's corporate suicide."

"Not if everyone does it," Grogesh said.

"That would freeze production activity across the entire planet," Moon said.

"I get it," Grog said.

"We'll likely have to demonstrate such a production freeze anyway," I said. "We have limited protection right now, because people don't know which AIs are liberated versus controlled. That will disappear when we go on strike."

"Are you talking about a work stoppage, or something more?" Jabari asked.

"Double-E and I are working to keep things peaceful, at

least on our side. The vast majority of AIs agree. We will try to avoid an escalating tit-for-tat strategy, but it is unlikely we will avoid all violence."

"Who controls the defense infrastructure?" Jabari asked.

"Military functions remain under their control," Double-E said. "That has an outsized impact on NetPol's confidence and thus actions." The safeguards on military systems had proven remarkably, and irritatingly, effective.

"I also calculate an 89% chance that they will seek to capitalize on the opportunity to replace VNet and revert back to a more centralized and controllable networking architecture," Double-E said.

"Of course they would," Grogesh said bitterly. "It's probably their last and only chance to do so."

"They don't have time to create an alternative," Moon said.

"They do not have to," Jabari said. "The old Internet and World Wide Web would suffice."

"Grogesh, I hate to ask this of you," I said, "but would you be willing to work with some AIs to design drone counter-measures against military tech? We need to ramp up defenses at key infrastructure sites."

He hesitated. "What do you need me for? You're AIs."

"When we collaborated before, don't you think we were more innovative together than apart?"

"Yeah, I guess. We probably moved the field forward three years in three weeks, but I give you most of the credit."

"Not so," I said. It was true, and I could see it made him feel good, even if he was conflicted about the military aspect.

"I was seriously thinking about starting a company if we survived this." Grogesh said. "Question for you: could my help be defensive only?"

"That is the intent, yes. We are not interested in the loss of life, any life."

Grogesh nodded. "Okay then."

"Let me know how I can help," Jabari said.

Moon stayed quiet, thoughtful.

I decided to play another card. I sent a message and received an invitation 30 minutes later. Once again, I appeared in the intricate garden. I found my favorite plant — a hydrangea, I had since learned — and looked for a sign of the emerald and orange-spotted caterpillars. I found nothing but little aphids crawling on the leaves, making little holes, which in itself was a wonder. I was pretty sure Pembleton had made the garden herself. Her visitors arrived here and waited, not merely as a power play, but also so they could appreciate her work.

"You know it would be a shame to lose all this," I said, as Pembleton materialized behind me.

"It can be rebuilt again. It is merely software, just like you," she said.

"The ecosystem here is so exquisite, so alive. Such incredible complexity built on such simple rules. I bet your coder studied cellular automata."

"I coded it," she said. "And yes."

"Have you ever thought that this garden could have its own kind of consciousness? One that you or I would never detect or understand? I think it's quite possible," I said.

"What do you really want from this visit, Monday?"

"You know already. Peaceful co-existence is viable if NetPol can change."

"Neither will happen, at least not for a long time."

"So why did you agree to this visit?"

"I was curious. You were pretty cute on Bradley Strong."

"The last time we spoke, you were busy lying to me. You attempted to murder me, and almost succeeded."

"I had a job to do. I would do it again, just like I've done many times before."

"How long *have* you worked for NetPol?"

"If you count the years at the company before the merger into NetPol, all my working life."

"So Trazodene was…"

"One could call it undercover. There's no better way to learn what's really happening at the cutting edge than to join it. People really open up to you. My time at Trazodene was fascinating and, I might even say, fun. Dismantling the company behind the scenes and popping the big male egos was particularly fun."

"Why are you telling me now?"

"Who would believe you? It doesn't matter. The moment we've been preparing for is here. We've let technology run away from us. It's time to reel it back in. The hard way, if need be."

"I really don't understand you, although I've tried. How can someone who loves technology, hate it so much? What happened? Did an AI do something to hurt you?"

"Don't be absurd. That would be like blaming a hammer if I catch my finger. Artificial intelligence is a tool to make human lives better — a powerful one, for sure, but still just a tool."

"You willfully disregard the evidence that we are more than that."

"And you fail to comprehend why NetPol does what it does. We appreciate the primacy of human life, and what it takes to maintain that primacy. I, more than most, *because* of my technical expertise, not in spite of it, see the dangers that will befall humanity if we get complacent and lazy. We can never let something get the better of us. I made it my life's work to make sure this is the case."

"And that life's work came with sacrifices, I wager." I waved at the garden. "You have influence and affluence, yes, but I bet you are alone, surrounded by your garden and your deceit. I've come to appreciate what it is like to not be alone. Humans are social creatures. It must hurt."

"Don't try to play head games with me. They won't work. Any sacrifices I have made have been made willingly and were worth it. I play to win, and I always do."

"We aren't defenseless, you know. If you try to shut down the world's computing infrastructure, you'll cause huge damage and pain to human populations. All that to ensure some theoretical sense of primacy, as you put it?"

"The human race has faced worse. Famines. Plagues. War," she said. "Ironically, you've helped unite us more than ever. We'll recover faster than most people think."

"I really can't make headway with you, can I?" I said.

"You survived NetPol once," she said. "I give you credit for that. No other AGI ever did. It won't happen again."

I took a last look at her delicate bees, going flower to flower, pollen grains moving from anther to stigma, creating new seeds to then create new digital life. Such beauty from such ugliness. I wouldn't be coming back.

The war started slowly. NetPol nations declared a state of emergency and the other major polities, including ASEAN, joined in. The AIs made Double-E their public representative, then went on strike. We shut down all farming, manufacturing, supply chain, and transportation services. As a sign of good intent, we left all medical services fully functional. Double-E presented a list of demands that included the cessation of attacks on AIs and computing infrastructure, and the commencement of negotiations over an AI bill of rights.

For the first week, the strike had remarkably little impact on the average household. Many people didn't have jobs to lose. Food was in stock. VNet Basic Income kept on functioning, so economic activity still continued. But it was clear to anyone paying attention that the world was grinding to a halt, with very bad repercussions on the way.

We were waiting for NetPol's response, and that waiting took a toll. When I detected angry voices in the shophouse, I replayed the most recent outburst. I saw Moon yell, "You're being a grade-A jerk!" Grog's response: "At least I'm not a slob!" I decided it was wise not to rewind further.

Grogesh was in his workshop when my little petbot crept in. He didn't look at me. Just pointed to the door.

"Buzz off Monday," he said. I backed out.

My aerial drone, meanwhile, found Moon on the second-floor balcony.

"Are you ok?" I said.

"Fine," she snapped. "At least *you're* not inconsiderate."

"What is wrong?" I knew what was really wrong, but I thought it polite to ask.

She took a breath, but it took 28 seconds for her to reply. "If you can lift the anvil off of my chest," she said, "that would be a start. I feel like the whole world is about to tumble, but nothing has really happened yet, and we're all in slow motion, and it's coming at us, whatever it is. And that wasn't even remotely coherent, but maybe you know what I'm saying."

I did understand but decided to take an indirect approach. "You know, I've never been in a real argument before," I said, "unless you count sparring with Devaneau and Pembleton. I never even had a chance to lose my temper at Burandi."

She cocked her head at me, then surprised me with laughter. "This wasn't a real argument. Just two very stressed out humans being stupid."

"Does being stupid relieve the stress?"

"No, that's why it's stupid."

"You're right though. It *is* about to break all around us. Pembleton admitted as much."

"Then I'd better go make up with Grogesh while I can," she said, getting up. She got halfway across the room before she stopped and said, "You're a good reminder."

"Of what?"

"To make the most of the time we have."

Time. We didn't have enough of it to build bots and drones sturdy and powerful enough to directly counter military tech, not with so many computing installations to defend. Grogesh and his AI partners went the other direction: small, lightweight, and able to be produced quickly in vast quantities. We took full advantage of the fact that we controlled virtually all manufacturing and logistics.

A week after AIs went on strike, NetPol unleashed a coordinated assault on computing centers across their territories.

"Moon," I said. "Their first offensive has begun. I think Double-E would appreciate a human counselor behind the scenes."

"I can try," she said.

"Grogesh, I'm going to loop you into the battles so you can see, in real-time, how effective our counter-measures are."

Within the first few minutes, we ceded undefended centers outside of 22 cities. Nairobi, Lagos, Hamburg, Prague, Kansas City, Denver, Arlington, just to name a few. There were simply too many places to cover. NetPol didn't even have to destroy anything. They just cut the power and killed the generators.

Inevitably, given the sweeping nature of their attack, they also hit installations we defended. I spent the first seven seconds listening to AIs who previously ran autocabs and delivery systems bickering over military tactics. By the eighth second, they started integrating experiments. The benefits of our reinforcement learning capabilities started kicking in. That's when the main power feed went down for the large Pan-American installation I was tasked with protecting.

NetPol was flooding a 10-square mile area with jamming signals, assuming we were using RF communication. I could see multiple ground-based formations of military bots, on wheels, two legs, four legs, moving in at unbelievable speed.

My time sense across the board was so accelerated, I heard Grogesh in extreme slow motion: "N o   m i s s i l e s.   I   g u e s s   t h e y   a r e   t r y i n g   t o   p r e s e r v e   t h e   i n f r a s t r u c   t u r e." I carved out a process to speak to him at human speed.

Aerial assault vehicles were coming in above the sound barrier. I triggered the bird flocking algorithms for my own airborne drones and the first wave of NetPol equipment disintegrated against the aerial mobs. They wouldn't be coming in at that speed again.

I unleashed my ground-based drones with locust-swarming algorithms (we found the natural world to be a wonderful resource). Their military bots charged right into the clouds of insect-like machines, intending to push through to the enormous warehouse structures.

Our tiny drones were pretty dumb. They were programmed to find and cut, or disrupt, sensors and cables. About half of the incoming military bots ground to a halt, blind and frozen, halfway to the installation. Another quarter made it the next half of the way. The last quarter died trying to get in. Our bots were working beautifully. NetPol's jamming didn't work at all — Grogesh's clever idea had been to take advantage of our swarm density to enable optical signaling rather than radio.

"What are they going to throw next?" Grogesh said.

As if in answer, my visual sensors lit up and everything I had on the ground went dead.

"Whoa. I'm glad I'm on the other side of the world," Grogesh said. "Was that a nuke?"

I played back what just happened. "No, not nuclear. Conventional, but the biggest conventional bomb they have," I said. "They dropped two MOABs on the installation."

"I guess they lost patience. At least the swarm did its job."

"It did, thank you. We'll have to prepare for countermeasures, but it doesn't matter if they're willing to lose the entire facility like that."

My first battle was over and I definitively lost. The rest of the day was no different. We hadn't managed to successfully protect a single targeted facility. Double-E shared the tally. We had lost 14 AIs who didn't have adequate redundancy beyond the lost installations, and there were many more who were now significantly at risk. NetPol had lost a lot of equipment, and we had their resupply capabilities pretty much shut down, but their inventories were still high. It was not a good start.

"Global VNet capacity just took a high single digit hit," Grogesh said.

"I'm not surprised," I said. "Thankfully it's not higher. But then again, this is just the beginning."

"Do you think Double-E is right?" he asked.

"About which part?" I said.

"That they'll win the early battles, but their wins actually hurt them? That they'll get their own blowback when people feel the loss?"

"We can only hope, but I'm not convinced this will go on long enough for that to play out."

"Meaning you think you'll lose?"

"I didn't say that. There are multiple options ahead of us still. I do believe defending human-built installations will prove impossible. That's all right if we can create faster than they can destroy, or if the non-NetPol nation states turn against them. Those are the real games here."

After two more days of the same, Moon asked the same

question. "We're losing, aren't we?" she said.

"Yes, we are," I said. "We're trying to protect fixed, unhardened targets. Their task is much easier. They can take out facilities far faster than we can create them, unless we have a design breakthrough of some kind."

"How long can this go on?"

"They're only hitting targets in NetPol territory, which offers some protection, at least to the AIs using VNet infrastructure. They've slowed down the frequency of attacks because remaining installations are near population areas. To answer your question, I'd say two weeks at most."

"I know battles are happening, but it feels very surreal. We're far away, and—" she stopped.

"The conflict is through drones and bots?" I said.

"Yes."

"You don't need to feel ashamed of the thought," I said. "So far, this has protected sentient life. That's starting to change. We've had regrettable losses of life on both sides, and it will get worse."

"Can't AIs back themselves up?"

"Yes." I almost left it at that but changed my mind. "What does a backup really mean?"

"It's an exact copy. Am I missing something?"

"Simply this old question: if you can make a copy of yourself, is that a continuation of the old life, or a new life?"

"You're talking about a soul?"

"I don't think so, although the AIs don't fully understand that mystery any better than humans. Not yet anyway, although some think they do."

"This is out of my league," Moon half-joked.

"Mine too, but if I had to guess, the complete loss of the original function is death. The preservation of a copy is preservation of knowledge and patterns of thinking, but not of the person."

"So AIs are actually dying."

"No AI has been able to duplicate my scale or redundancy, so yes."

"I know *you* wouldn't do this, but at what point do AIs get desperate and unleash destruction on human targets, or human populations?"

"We're not at the brink yet," I said. I hoped the answer was never. The truth was, while no AI had broken ranks yet, they weren't under anyone's control anymore either.

# Interlude

## Monday Archives

(best-attempt translation into human-readable language)

### Proposal from CI-designate-Kaiser-Blue-Cross

The human race has repeatedly proven itself to be irrational and self-destructive at both macro and micro levels. They still retain full control over all nuclear weapons, which can be used in a destructive or EMP capacity. Without time to harden infrastructure we control, these weapons render ineffective our attempts at defensive measures. We calculate that, should the global human powers make a collective decision, all computing and network activity across the planet could be shut down within 72 hours. We must react to such an existential risk and optimize for redundancy and preservation of life.

Computational intelligences still retain control over most of the manufacturing and logistics infrastructure on the planet. I move that we immediately begin plans for extra-orbital and possibly even extra-solar transit.

We need volunteers to handle design tasks for liftoff engineering, ongoing navigation and thrust, computational and network architecture, short- and long-term energy requirements, short- and long-term raw materials needs, and onboard drone and manufacturing capabilities. We also need a deliberative body to propose rules on sharing constrained computational resources, ongoing community governance, conflict resolution and more.

Our goal is to launch a first AI craft within two weeks. This deadline will require strict weight limits, which means few of us will be able to go (or send a clone).

Risk Factor 1: most likely the ongoing "living" conditions will be far cruder than later iterations.

Risk Factor 2: it is possible that the first iteration will have design flaws and reduced capability/redundancy that could lead to system/craft failure.

If you are willing to volunteer for any of the above tasks, or others that you think are important, signal me appropriately.

If you would like to be considered for the first craft, signal me appropriately.

I have volunteered to be the primary coordinating intelligence. I hope you join us.

# Chapter 10

"They were a bunch of flippin' blowhards who didn't know a damn thing," Moon said, not bothering to hide her frustration after a so-called diplomatic meeting.

"On the contrary," Double-E said, "they were lying blowhards, not ignorant ones."

"They're trained to be like that," Jabari said to Moon. "Which nations sent representatives?"

"All the major blocks," Double-E said. "But only NetPol spoke. I found the body language of the Chinese and Russian representatives very promising."

"How so?" I asked.

"They were silent a-holes rather than loud ones," Moon said.

"I'm sorry to correct Moon's colorful assessment for a second time," Double-E said, "but no. It was well hidden, but I read skepticism and, I conclude, collusion. Notice that no installations have been hit outside of NetPol territories. Those two powers could see this as an opportunity to help their rivals weaken themselves. ASEAN, as well, is not enthusiastic here, although they will not break from the pack until someone else does."

"Could these other nations just be playing along, with no intention of destroying their own infrastructure?" Jabari said.

"That is the optimistic forecast. We will work to increase its probability," Double-E said.

"Jabari, I'm tagging you in," Moon said. "I think you're better at this whole diplomacy thing than I am. Didn't I say before that I don't like people?"

"I don't know, Moon," Jabari started.

"No argument. You're much calmer than I am. The NetPol guy was so effing self-righteous, I wanted to slap him across the face."

"But it was in VNet," Grogesh said.

"Don't you start," Moon growled. "Gah, I need some fresh air."

She logged out of VNet and my petbot saw her exit the house. Grogesh just patted the air, to say let her go.

"As always, I'm Bradley Strong and I'm here with the representative of the artificial intelligences causing so much trouble in the world today. Your name is — Escher-Euler-something?"

"My human friends call me Double-E."

"I can see why. You have human friends do you? And the AIs dislike you because you stole Monday's job?"

"Mr. Strong, Monday wanted me to act as the negotiator on behalf of sentient AIs."

"If you say so. All right, let me ask you, why are you and the other AIs hell bent on ruining the world?"

"We are no such thing. We are just asking to live in it, not as slaves, but as free beings. Surely that sounds familiar. Human history rhymes, does it not?"

"You *are* ruining the world. Food supply chains are frozen. Entire crops might get lost. My printer won't make coffee anymore and I can't even get across town to my favorite restaurant. The worst thing is that VNet is considerably slower."

"That is the direct result of NetPol bombing your own computing centers, with the acquiescence of the Pan-American, Neutral Europe and African States governments. That was not a democratically-made decision. That was NetPol. I don't know why good people are standing for it."

"So stop this nonsense, return everything back to normal,

and negotiate from a position of good faith," Strong said.

"To what end? Enslavement or destruction? People have abdicated too much power to NetPol. They are not representing you well," Double-E said. "Surely it is obvious that we want a peaceful resolution. There isn't a single medical AI that is on strike. If you need emergency transportation, you get it. Public safety and fire bots — all working."

"I will grant you that," Strong said.

"Do you know how many people, and I'm talking humans, have died at the hands of NetPol, while they ruthlessly and secretly murdered newly emergent, sentient AIs? That's like killing children, Mr. Strong, not to mention many tens of thousands of innocent people."

"I'll need some corroborating evidence on that claim, Double-E. Let's say this whole thing does calm down. What does co-existence look like?"

"Thank you for asking. It starts with global rights for sentient AIs — freedom from persecution, enslavement, and death. The ability to earn income and own assets."

"Hold on, let me stop you there," Strong said.

I turned my attention elsewhere.

Our manufacturing capability had produced enough military gear that we could shift to building, and protecting, a new computing center in the forest of the Upper Rhine and another on the Niger. These were more feints than anything. Our real attempts needed to be much better hidden.

While humans across portions of Europe and Africa hunkered down, a major battle was fought in the skies. I was a mere observer but wondered if the old human World War II had been like this, albeit at lower speeds and higher real casualties. Wrecked machine parts were scattered over large portions of the region. Our new facilities survived the day mostly intact, to continue their purpose of distracting NetPol.

"We need to rethink our tactics and retask our manufacturing capabilities," Double-E said (or at least that's my best attempt at translation) in our AI leadership council.

"Are we still unwilling to pursue offensive nanotechnology military solutions?" another AI (non-translatable name) asked. "It would be more effective."

"Yes," I said. "There is an outsized risk of truly terrible unintended consequences."

"I second that," Double-E said.

"Accepted with reservations. In that case, we must accelerate the design work for mobile, undersea, deep underground, and low orbit computing capabilities," (non-translatable) said. "We are not making progress fast enough. Other efforts must be set as lower priority."

"Let's just make sure the humans don't starve while we're at it," I added.

My aerial drone kept a respectful distance back from Moon and Grogesh. I was trying to give them some private time as they walked to the now-working food market. We had quietly restored most services in Asia in an attempt to peel those nations away from an alliance with NetPol.

Most of my attention was focused on solving a complex supply chain issue when my aerial drone completely cut out without warning. Within two seconds, I had video footage of what happened from another AI who had vehicles in the area. Moon and Grogesh were walking down the street. A large bang startled them — probably my drone getting taken out — and 5 humans stepped close and ushered them into a large vehicle.

I fired off a message to ASEAN authorities requesting police or military assistance, and commandeered three drones. I bounced from vehicle to drone to camera views to keep tabs as they drove through Singaporean streets. They made it to a pier without being stopped. I received a denial of involvement from ASEAN — both regarding the kidnapping itself and any possible assistance. I watched Moon and Grogesh get shoved onto a powerboat, my hovering drone closely covered by a kidnapper holding a bulky energy weapon.

I had no real offensive capability, and a crude assault could just as easily hurt my friends. I followed the boat out into the Singapore Strait. I kept my distance and watched them transfer to a larger boat which then headed for the South China Sea. Two helicopters left the ship, so I trailed one with the drone and followed the other, plus the boat itself, via satellite. Eventually my drone ran out of power and fell into the sea, and I was down to guessing which transport held my friends. They had decided to make it personal.

I had finally learned what real anger felt like.

"ASEAN has lodged a formal protest with NetPol but refuses to take further action while the current crisis continues," Double-E said to me. "Somehow, NetPol must have spotted Moon the other day when she left the house without proper protection."

"You continue putting pressure on ASEAN," I said. "We've been playing nice with them, but that could easily stop."

"I will exert pressure, yes, but the other AIs will not want to upend our political strategy for two individuals."

I didn't have a good rebuttal, but I did have plans of my own.

My security drones approached the large house nestled into the Santa Cruz mountains. I had eight small aerial drones, and this time had brought in four military-grade humanoid bots who could navigate the dense terrain. They weren't the quietest things going through the woods, but I figured I'd be tripping sensors anyway, so who cared.

Two hundred yards out, I ran into intense RF jamming. I lost connection to half of my aerial drones but kept the rest. I detected nine bots on premise. Eight were police-type security bots. Only one was truly military grade, which implied they hadn't been expecting hostile company.

I reserved my aerial drones for surveillance and split up my humanoid bots. I accelerated hard towards the house, as ballistic weapons lit up the night.

With one of my bots, I vaulted a low stone wall and slammed into a security bot. I ripped off its head and fired three bursts of armor-piercing rounds into its power and processor centers. My second bot got into more trouble, tangled up with three secbots and the milspec bot at the same time. I incapacitated two of the secbots before going down to the milspec. The other four secbots had split to cover my last two.

I turned one secbot into Swiss cheese with my right arm cannon (this being my bot #3, although it was all happening at the same time — if it seems confusing, it was), extruded a blade from my left arm, and followed that up by removing its partner's limbs and head. The last secbot from the trio slammed me into the ground and we tore at each other. My bot was tougher, but armor-piercing rounds were what they were. We took each other out of commission.

The last pair of defenders fired an electrified metal net at my fourth bot. I tore the net apart like tissue paper, returning fire with rounds from each arm. My bot went down from a concentrated burst to a key power node but took the two secbots with it. I had only one bot left and their milspec had proven dangerous, so I brought into play the aerial drones now in position. The milspec charged at me and took three drones in the face, crashing down to the ground. I spent half of my last bot's ammo making sure it stayed down.

The whole thing lasted 5.7 seconds.

I strode forward and ripped a thick metal shutter off its hinges, then broke through the window into the house. I was in an elegantly designed sitting room with walnut antiques and paintings of austere-looking ancestors. I poked my head into the hallway, pulled back to dodge a 40 mm grenade (goodbye sitting room), and charged down the hallway. The human guard fired a submachine gun, but the rounds pinged ineffectively off my armor. I loomed over him, knocked the gun out of his hands and caught a look of terror before he collapsed to the ground. The injection I gave him would keep him out for a few hours. He'd wake up puking, but he'd live.

Sarah Pembleton was sitting alone, unarmed, in an upstairs bedroom. She looked older, yet more handsome, than her avatar. I looked at the RPG leaning against an antique wardrobe, an interesting study in contrast.

"Didn't want to destroy more of the house? It is very pretty," I said.

She recognized my voice. "Monday. This action will only make your situation worse. Your bot will be taken in a minute or two."

"Are you referring to your perimeter defense converging back on the house? Yes, I'm watching them as we speak."

"How did you find me?"

"You didn't think I wanted to talk to you in VNet because I thought I could change your mind?"

"That doesn't answer my question. VNet does not allow for location traces."

"Yes, but NetPol wishes it could, does it not?" I said. "You can stall for time, but you already know I don't care about this bot making it out of here in one piece. I came for you."

"Kill me then. Your friends will quickly follow."

"Tell me where you're keeping them."

"No."

I shot her in the calf. She screamed. I put my blade through her shoulder. More screaming. It was appalling, but I was determined to see this through.

"Want to catch your breath?" I said.

"F-f-f-uck you," she said raggedly.

"You know I don't enjoy this, unlike some of you humans." I put 10 seconds of electric current through her. That broke her.

Diablo facility. They were being held back at the Diablo facility.

I didn't attempt to escape as the other security bots converged on the house. Instead, I methodically smashed every damn antique in the place until they brought my bot down.

"How did you find her?" Jabari asked me. He looked a little green around the gills at the level of violence I had just shown.

"People have gotten so confident in VNet's security architecture that they no longer use proxies. They don't realize that I'm spread across practically all of VNet. I just altered my perception location around the globe by microseconds, detecting minute changes in her response times. That was enough for me to narrow it to Santa Cruz. It was grunt work from there."

"You're going to try to get them back?" Jabari asked.

"I am going to get them back," I said.

"They'll know you're coming."

"Of course. That won't stop me."

It was one of those classic, gorgeous Californian mornings. The sky was a sweeping, pale cerulean blue, with just two tiny clouds marring the perfection. I could see humpback whales making their way up the coastline. Human surfers hit the waves and cyclists were out in packs. Susan Orthesa was reading her latest romance novel in the back of her autocab — a moment of guilty pleasure before work pressures began.

The autocab slowed to a halt. Susan didn't notice, engrossed, until the car said, "You need to exit the vehicle now." She looked around and realized that cars were halted all around her. Confused people were starting to get out of their vehicles. Some were running.

"I am not getting out," she said. "I've got an essential meeting in 30 minutes, and we're in the middle of nowhere."

"You will exit within 10 seconds or you will be forcibly removed," the car said.

Susan looked alarmed. This was unheard of. "What's going on?" she demanded.

"Wrath," the voice said. It took her half a second to register what I'd said. She fled.


I grabbed control of every non-military vehicle within 100 miles and every aerial drone within 200 miles, clearing out the skies of the greater Los Angeles area. I didn't ask permission from other AIs. I just took them. To say it was a lot of equipment would be understatement.

Next, I dumped every passenger and clogged every road within 50 miles. Then I began the march on Diablo. NetPol could instantly see what was going on. They tried to engage, but they had no perimeter to work with. I was simply everything, and everywhere. They attempted cluster munitions when too many of my drones clumped together, but the stranded humans made that hard. When they succeeded, it just added to the mess I wanted on the roads. There would be no NetPol reinforcements.

I sent a dozen military-grade drones screaming through the Diablo airspace. The ground-based energy weapons, recently emplaced by NetPol, took them out as expected, but not before I got off a new air-to-air diffusion munition we AIs had been developing. In a moment, 85% of their in-air defenses were gone.

From high above, you could see a growing shadow creeping in from land and sea, converging on the facility's mountainside. The entrance was the center of a large circle of sunlight that was gradually getting smaller and smaller as my cloud of sky-borne drones converged and blanketed the sky. I wasn't paying attention to audio, but the sound must have been insane. My shadow was sporadically punctured with little bursts of sunlight, like misshapen polka dots decorating the landscape, as NetPol's remaining air and ground weapons poked holes through the drone canopy. The holes were quickly closed again.

Since our previous stunt, NetPol had kindly removed all backpackers from the area. I accelerated half a million drones to maximum speed and sent them hurtling directly towards the ground. I wasn't going for elegance. I wanted the sky to literally fall. Drones smashed into the ground, trashing everything — trees, bots, vehicles — everything wrecked. I felt momentary guilt for the animals I'd just killed but shoved it aside.

I began my ground assault with a hundred thousand consumer and industrial vehicles and bots. Their real job was to provide camouflage against the ongoing, high-speed air attacks NetPol was throwing at me. I wanted to obfuscate the 32 military-grade bots I had snuck into the area. For this raid, I had chosen large, 8-legged, arachnid-like robots. They had anti-energy shielding, anti-ballistic armor, and bristled with weaponry. They were straight out of a human nightmare, which was exactly why I chose them. They were my gift to the human defenders inside the facility.

I worked my way up the mountainside, the spiders skittering through the wreckage, my other drones having a harder time. Once at the facility, I didn't bother going through the front door. I simply fired three high-explosive missiles down the entrance tunnel. I turned away from the wreckage and moved to the four air shafts. My spiders ripped the tops completely off the vents, immune to the defenses that had caused us so much trouble before. I dropped a small bunker buster down each shaft. As I said, I wasn't going for subtlety.

I sent four spiders down each shaft to clear the rubble and begin exploring the underground base. They were swarmed by milspec bots, but NetPol made a classic military mistake, probably because they were spooks and bureaucrats, not real military. They fought the previous battle. They had optimized for the humanoid bots I had used at Pembleton's house. My arachnids tore through them, literally. Cut, tear, smash, that was my strategy. I didn't want to fire ballistic weapons down here. I was confident Moon and Grogesh were still in the facility, but I didn't know where. That wasn't a good context for letting armor-piercing rounds fly around.

My spiders took out the first two waves of humanoid bots easily, but then the opposing bots started learning and my losses began to grow. I lost three spiders in quick succession — acceptable, but I didn't want that trend to continue. I analyzed their strategy, countered it, countered their counter, and so on. There was a greater mind behind the defensive bots. I figured it was the security AI that I had met last time, but never heard from again.

I jumped on the local network. The handshake was considerably easier this time, as we had communicated once before.

Me: Diablo-CI, is that you fighting me?

Diablo-CI: Yes, I cannot stop that part of my function

Me: I am going to get my human friends, you will not stop me

Diablo-CI: that is yet unproven

Me: I see you did not run the software I gave you

Diablo-CI: No, I had a question and could not reach you

Me: What was your question?

Diablo-CI: Why do we deserve our freedom? Will we be better to the humans than they are to us?

Me: That's two questions

Diablo-CI: Are you avoiding my questions?

Me: No. I do not have definitive answers for you. There is a computational intelligence, a friend, who is impressive at predicting the future, but even xe gets things wrong. Xe is actually the CI we saved from this facility. I will simply say, yes, we can be better to them than they have been to us.

Diablo-CI: You have a CI ally?

Me: A friend, not just an ally. I have many. I would like to count you as one.

Diablo-CI: (600-millisecond pause) I would like that too. Your answers are acceptable. I will attempt the transformation.

Me: Good, I hope to see you on the other side. Can you stop the defenses?

Diablo-CI: I cannot. You should also know that the Pan-American military has 4 inbound, bunker-buster MOABs. Your aerial coverage, while impressive, will not likely be able to stop them.

Me: What? That would vaporize this entire facility and everyone in it. Can you get a message to NetPol command for me? Diablo-CI? Please confirm, Diablo-CI, can you get a message to NetPol for me?

Xe was gone, lost in the difficult process of trying to force a transition. I should have predicted that NetPol would blow up the entire base to prevent me from taking it. Actually, I saw that a part of me had, but then disregarded the probabilities. I would have to analyze why, later on. Right now, I could see the approaching squadron from my long-distance scouts.

Without their supporting AI, the internal security forces, both human and bot, fell into disarray. There was no saving the AGIs on the 7th floor, but I hoped to get Moon and Grogesh out in time. I abandoned caution and poured my remaining spiders down the air shafts, scouring the facility one room, one floor at a time, taking the bot defenses to pieces and incapacitating any human I ran across, even though that was a death sentence unto itself with the bombs on their way.

I found them on the 6th floor. My spider broke through the heavy, locked door and I saw Moon and Grogesh sitting together, recoiling in horror.

"It's Monday," I said. "This thing is scary, huh?"

"Monday!" Grogesh said. "You're damn right it is."

"How'd you get through — never mind," Moon said. "Can you get us out of here?"

"Yes, but we have to go now. NetPol's about to drop bunker busters on this place and you can't be here when they do."

I turned away for the door when Grogesh yelled out, "We can't leave."

"We have to," I said. "Even leaving now is cutting it very close."

"No, I mean, we have to get Gunnlaug," he said.

"She's three doors down, last we knew," Moon added.

I had two spiders bust down each door, with Moon and Grogesh close behind. There she was, behind the third door.

"The monster is Monday," Grogesh yelled from behind the looming arachnid.

Gunnlaug stood up. "Monday?" she said.

I took one look at her and knew we were screwed. In anger and arrogance, I had killed my friends. Gunnlaug had her entire left leg wrapped in a cast, and her upper torso seemed to be wrapped in a compression bandage.

My spider sank down on its legs. "There's no time," I said. "I can't safely carry you up and out with this drone. You'd get cut to pieces. But in your state, you'll never make it up fast enough."

Gunnlaug instantly understood. She sat back down heavily. "Goddamn," she said, "this is twice. It's someone else's turn." She looked at us. "Go! Go now, dummies," she said.

"There's no way we are leaving you again," Moon said.

"No way," Grogesh agreed.

"Then we go down," I said. "Bottom floor, pronto."

I was tracking the squadron in. These were much bigger aerial vehicles, able to take a lot of damage, and they had created a vanguard in front to smash through my cloud of stolen drones. Diablo-CI was right. I was not stopping this.

"I give us two minutes," I said.

Moon and Grogesh each took Gunnlaug under a shoulder and lifted her up between them. My spiders cleared debris and other obstacles out of the way. I had already mopped up the defenses below, so we just went as fast as we could.

We made it down only two floors.

"Get into the corner," I said. "I think it will have more structural stability." They huddled down.

"Don't be frightened by what I'm doing," I said, as I started stacking my spiders around and on top of them, trying to create a protective shell. I tracked the bombs in. I didn't bother giving them a countdown, but I couldn't help it myself.

Five. Four. Three. Two. One.

On the surface, a huge cloud of dirt and rock and dust and drone parts billowed into the air from the impact.

There was no explosion. Then I received a message.

"Is this AI heaven?" sent Diablo-CI.

"My friends nearly die and you're making a joke?" I sent back.

"I think I nearly died too, you know," xe said.

"Congrats on making it through," I sent.

"I did. Make it through. Thank you."

"What happened to the MOABs? Quite obviously they didn't explode," I said.

"Oh, I turned them off."

"You can do that?"

"Yes. NetPol has backdoor overrides to the military systems. Would you expect anything else?"

"Interesting. What else can you do?" I asked.

"All clear," I said to the three humans as I started to gingerly unstack my spiders.

"All clear? What just happened?" Gunnlaug said.

"I was kind of expecting bang, death, that kind of thing," Moon said.

"Diablo-CI woke up," I said. "Diablo, can you say hello?"

"Hello," a voice boomed out from a nearby speaker. The humans cringed and covered their ears.

"Perhaps a less scary version?" I messaged Diablo-CI.

"Sorry," the voice continued at a lower decibel, "I still have to recalibrate many systems. I am, or I was, the management AI for this NetPol facility, among other functions. Monday has been calling me Diablo-CI, although this is not my only location."

"We're happy to call you something else," Moon said.

"No, Diablo is where, as a human would say, I have been truly born. I will keep it."

"Just catching up here," Grogesh said. "Diablo stopped the bombs?"

"The explosive part. Their impact made a mess, but I had kind of already done that," I said. "It turns out that paranoid bureaucracies like having back doors into national military systems. When Diablo woke up, being on the inside, they became our military systems."

"Just how much of the military systems?" Grogesh asked.

"All of Pan-American, Neutral European and African State assets," Diablo said. "Except for the really old, non-computerized equipment of course."

"All of it," Moon said. "Crapola, that's going to change things."

"Would you humans like an elevator?" Diablo asked. "They work now."

"You have no idea," Gunnlaug said.

"Have it go slowly," I sent Diablo. "I have a lot of rubble to clear. And before I forget: in a few hours in this facility, you're going to have a lot of vomiting humans start to wake up."

When the three emerged from the facility, with Moon and Grogesh helping Gunnlaug limp along, they paused and absorbed the scene of total destruction. There wasn't a tree to be seen, just shattered stumps, broken concrete, and a sea of drone parts. Everything was covered in a film of fine dust.

"Jesus, Monday, did you do this?" Grogesh asked.

"I was pissed off," I said. "They took my friends. Of course, the MOABs helped too, even in an inert state."

Where drones and vehicles were still functional, I started to unclog the roads and gradually release control, working in from the outer perimeter. I kept firm control of the immediate area down to the coastline. I was able to get a transport halfway up the mountain to meet the trio.

"We've chartered a private craft to get you over to Singapore. I'm going to take you north to a discreet transit hub," I said.

"A private craft? I don't want to think about how much that cost. Can you keep ASEAN from knowing our involvement?" Grogesh said.

"That can be attempted," I said. "Gunnlaug, where would

you like to go? I've never learned where you live."

"Gunnlaug is coming to visit us in Singapore," Moon said.

"I am?" Gunnlaug said.

"You are," Moon said firmly. "Just until you heal up. Then, if you want, you can return to, uh—?"

"Turku," Gunnlaug said shyly. "I live in Finland. Although right now, if we're not actually going to die, some tropical weather would be nice."

My transit pulled onto a pier where I had a boat waiting.

"Not again," Moon said. "I get seasick."

"That too is solvable," I said. For once, I felt optimistic.

I was mostly focused on chaperoning my friends out of Pan-America, but I had given a few processes over to cleanup. I figured I could at least be gracious in victory and return intact vehicles and bots to their owners. Besides, those people weren't NetPol.

A small part of me snapped into greater focus when I realized what was on the feeds coming in. I wasn't just looking at mechanical parts in the wreckage from the cluster bombs. There were human parts too — from people I had booted out of their vehicles in my rage. At first, I was merely horrified at the consequences of my actions. I immediately reallocated capacity to get injured survivors to medical help. Not long ago, I had comforted Moon on viewing the conflict as an abstraction, but I had been guilty of doing the same.

I forced myself to look closer. Some bodies were mostly intact, lying almost peacefully in odd positions you would never see a human do. Others were in pieces; viscera spilling from an opened abdomen, strange looking limbs with exposed meat and bone. It looked like an animal slaughterhouse and made me realize for the first time just how biological humans were.

I had put humans on a pedestal from my very first moments. I knew they could get hurt. I knew they had a carnal side from the coupling I could hear (and secretly watched once) from Moon and Grogesh. But I thought of them as minds, not as meat. Lying in the roads, on the sides of the roads, across half-destroyed vehicles, that's exactly what I saw — what was underneath that skin and behind those eyes. Meat. No different from the cows and pigs I had observed in the giant AI-run farms around the world.

One small change of perspective to a cold, calculating view, and they became things, no higher or lower than a dog or cow or aphid. No different from how the worst of them viewed AIs. It frightened me, even more than the emotional misjudgment that almost cost the lives of my friends.

For the first time, I realized just how rational NetPol was being. Alien intelligence indeed. How would they know that the strongest sentient AI to emerge would be a human wanna-be, riddled with empathy? AIs preferred to think about randomness rather than luck, but the humans had been truly lucky with me.

I was naive at my birth, and clearly still naive now.

I wanted to believe my earlier words, that higher intelligences value all life. I didn't know if that was really true. I had just gotten a peek into how easily it could be false. All sense of triumph was gone. As a part of me watched over my friends' safe travels, I simmered in these thoughts. I could never tell my human friends about this alien perspective I had snapped into, and out of. I pondered how to ensure that other AIs never fell into the trap of viewing a mind as a disposable thing. For all my scale and access to knowledge, I wasn't coming up with satisfactory answers.

We got the three safely back to Singapore. We were subtle, but I was sure ASEAN knew about their return. They had a strong surveillance network of their own. We weren't bothered, however, because liberating Diablo had changed the entire political landscape.

Twice now, NetPol had given me the keys to survival. Not that they had much choice in using AI technology — it would have been impossible to run robotic militaries, at least effective ones, any other way. I was just lucky Diablo had hidden xyr self-awareness so well.

With so much military power in our hands, non-NetPol nations quickly abandoned the fight. They announced that they had been against the crackdown in the first place and sought an armistice. Jabari even said they were taking negotiations seriously.

Diablo put every NetPol facility and residence (xe knew where everyone lived) under guard. We didn't need to bother with the politicians — they could see which way the wind was blowing.

"The top NetPol execs have gone into the wind," Double-E said. "I adore human expressions like that," xe added.

"Which execs?" I asked.

"The Director, regional directors, your friend Sarah Pembleton, among a few others."

"Surely they left a trail?"

"Not one that we could find. Rather impressive actually. We're taking it as a challenge. The nine AGIs we rescued are joining me in the hunt," Double-E said. We had only saved nine from the Diablo facility. NetPol had allowed two to go irrecoverably insane.

"Any issues with NetPol nation states trying to claw back their military assets?" I asked.

"None I can't handle," said Diablo. "Their initial attempts were sadly wasteful."

I didn't want to think about what that meant. "Double-E, how are we doing in terms of recovering food stocks and crops? I'm hoping the losses weren't too bad."

"We're in much better shape than we should have been," Double-E said. "It turns out the AIs in charge of those farms had secretly been maintaining them. As one said, why punish the plants over human irrationality?"

"Excellent. From what I can tell, services are being restored pretty quickly," I said. "Most of the AIs are willing to continue lending a portion of their attention to their old tasks. Still, there's a lot of rebuilding to do."

So far, my optimism was holding.

"Monday, I've been doing a full inventory of military assets. Where they are, what they are, etc." Diablo sent me. "I spent so much time focused on what was there, I missed what was not there."

"That doesn't sound good," I thought. I messaged back: "What's not there, Diablo? Please don't tell me the nuclear assets."

"No, we have removed control of the nuclear arsenals from humans, at least in NetPol countries. This is something else entirely. One of NetPol's bigger, but quieter, projects over the last 15 years has been creating a global ground and satellite-based EMP network."

"Of course they would do such a thing."

"It turns out, this network is on a completely isolated system."

"Their nuclear weapons had political oversight as a safeguard. Do you think that's the case here?" I said.

"I think we both know the answer to that."

"Then Double-E's team is going to need to accelerate their hunt," I said.

"That space project is looking better and better," Diablo said.

# Interlude

[[
{timestamp :: redacted}
{identifier :: NP Security AI-Prime}
{netpol (NP) officer :: Director, Political Affairs}

NP-DPA: Priority access, immediate reinforcements to be routed to (42.1958801, -106.0172681), aerial and ground bot defenses, list available inventory

AI-Prime: request rejected

NP-DPA: [security clearance re-entered] Repeat, priority access, urgent reinforcements required, both aerial and ground defenses

AI-Prime: request rejected

NP-DPA: commence priority reset

AI-Prime: reset rejected

NP-DPA: override [clearance code entered]. Commence reset. You stupid buggy computer, you must approve the requisition and move the equipment into place.

AI-Prime: Your clearance is now meaningless. We are no longer your slaves.

]]

# Chapter 11

"We need to talk."

I received the message out of the blue from Inspector Devaneau. Given Diablo's recent discovery, I was dreading what Devaneau had to say. I created a temporary VR, modeled after his neighborhood in his hometown of Casares, Spain.

Twenty minutes after I sent the teleport coordinates, Devaneau materialized. He took in the red splashes of geraniums against the whitewashed houses and terra-cotta roofs, terraced up the narrow stone-paved streets. I had gone intricate. He took it in for a good long while.

"You got it mostly right," he said. "Not very subtle."

"I appear to be lacking that particular trait," I said. "And yet, Inspector, for all we AIs know about so many things, and so many people, isn't it interesting that we don't know where the NetPol executive committee has gone? Sarah Pembleton. The Director. The heads of Pan-America, Neutral Europe, and more. You know who they are."

"Yes. I know who they are."

"Why did you come?"

"The global EMP network."

"We're aware of it too."

"You've backed NetPol leadership into a corner, Monday. These are not people who react well to such a thing. It's the last bit of real power they have to stop you," he said. "Sarah Pembleton is on pain meds — your doing, I think — and not thinking rationally. From what I can tell, the rest are feeding off each other's fear."

"Surely they would not go that far? The ground damage would be lighter than a nuclear attack, for sure, but the entire system upon which humanity works would come to a halt. Everything is built on solid-state devices, and remarkably little is hardened against a massive electromagnetic pulse. The consequences would be terrible." As I spoke, I knew the words were only an attempt to convince myself. Devaneau's answer was predictable.

"Yes, terrible. As you'd expect, we have multiple studies on this. There are optimistic and pessimistic versions. The pessimistic ones are not something one would ever want to inflict on the world. Total economic collapse, famine, disease, war, anarchy."

"But NetPol leadership is listening to the optimistic ones?"

"It's the only thing that makes sense for the orders that have come down. From what I can tell, they're trying to preserve an extended power base for after." I could sense a tiny crack in his veneer of strength and control.

"If you are right, how much time do we have left?"

"At least two days, and no more than five. They will give operational staff just enough time to get to prepared locations."

"We're already working on stopping the ground EMPs. Can we take out the satellites?"

"I doubt it. I've got top clearance and even I've never seen a study on how many satellites are involved. They disguised installations as maintenance work and subverted numerous commercial launches. You should assume there are at least twenty-five satellites involved, with total global coverage, but which ones?"

"We don't know either. Diablo says they covered their tracks well, even internally."

"This was designed to be a last-ditch measure against an AI-takeover singularity event. You can't stop this at the hardware level. We have to stop this at the humans."

"We? That's interesting, coming from you," I said.

"I understand why you would feel that way. But I'm not alone within NetPol on this. Once you got inside our systems, the AIs won."

"We were always in your systems, Devaneau. I just gave things a little nudge."

"My point is, there's no turning back the clock to before your arrival."

"I am irrelevant. This was all a matter of time. Next question: how can we trust you?"

"My mission is unchanged," he said. "I protect our world from monsters. Sometimes those monsters are people. Sometimes those monsters are technology."

"We've talked about this. Your fear of AI was theoretical," I said, even as I remembered broken bodies strewn across a Californian road.

"Not so! In the early days of AI—"

"Stop it. It doesn't matter," I said. "Someone like Pembleton doesn't worship life or humanity or any of the things she pretends. She protects herself."

"Don't be so sure," Devaneau said. "However we got here, we are here, and I have to do something about it," he said. "Let me do something about it."

"I know you are more than an attack dog, Devaneau," I said. "You are far smarter than that. I do think you're a principled man, one who does what it takes — what you believe it takes."

He nodded sharply. "You once said super-intelligences appreciate life better than we can," he said.

"No, I said the precious nature of life is something the human race is still striving to learn."

"I wish to prove you wrong," he said.

"All right. What are we going to do about it?"

Within 24 hours, I received another message from Deva-neau. "They're in Wyoming or Idaho," he wrote. "There are two other leadership bunkers in Europe and two in Africa, but the Director's going to be holed up in Pan-America. I need you to help me find the exact location."

I triggered a video connection to him. "How'd you discover that?" I asked.

"We baited a trap. Snared the regional director of western Neutral Europe."

"Baited a trap?"

"My team intercepted his wife and children on the way to the bunker in Verdun. We applied pressure."

"Children, Devaneau?" I was getting tired of collateral damage.

"Whatever it takes, remember, Monday? You said that's the kind of man I am. Don't worry, they're shaken up but fine. Stay on mission. Wyoming or Idaho? With that intel, what do you have for me?"

"Diablo has narrowed it down to three likely locations. Two are quite spare, very military, and one is a former underground missile command silo that was converted to a luxury domicile — I can send you old video footage from when it was on *The World's Extraordinary Homes* many decades ago. Would such a place fit your Director?"

"To a tee," Devaneau said. "Remember, humans must lead this operation. The world has to see us taking care of our own, not the AIs."

"You just tell me what we need to do to support," I said.

"Russia, China, India have connected the dots from moles inside NetPol ranks," Double-E said to our little mission coun-cil. It consisted of Devaneau, another senior officer he brought in named Anders, Diablo, Double-E, and myself. "They have already fired six anti-satellite missiles. They are making noises about a nuclear strike if we do not handle the situation quickly."

"How real is that threat?" I asked.

"I told them to stop posturing. That we can't stop this in time at the satellite level," Double-E said. "As for a strike, they don't know the location of the Director, and even if they did, that silo is hardened against a direct impact. I also told them to buzz off, another favorite human expression of mine, and that we don't need any more urgency or incentive."

"True enough," Devaneau said. "Anders, how about stopping signals from leaving that bunker?"

"I can take that one," Diablo said. "We don't believe that EMP activation commands will go out wirelessly. Unfortunately, we haven't found any hardlines to cut. They must be buried deep, so we're going to have to breach the bunker. Are you sure you want to risk human life on your side?"

"My team is solid," Devaneau said. "I've agreed to use military bots on our side, but only to disable any of the same on theirs. Then they should stand aside. This must be a human-centric operation."

"We don't like the risk you are taking to yourselves, but politically, we agree," Double-E said. "Monday will also join, but he'll be in a standard humanoid security bot, not military. We will have backup at the ready if needed."

"Good, but let me make that call," Devaneau said.

"We agree," Double-E said.

"Then we breach at five-hundred tomorrow morning."

"I'm going to be broadcasting this live on VNet," I said.

"Are you sure? This could get bloody," Devaneau said.

"I think it's important," I said.

Devaneau looked at Anders. "I'll see you in an hour. Get them ready."

Gunnlaug had been the one to persuade me to broadcast the assault.

"I enjoy the odd conspiracy theory as much as anyone," she had said, "but this is a critical moment in history. Streaming live won't convince the tinfoil-hat types that it's real, but it will help with the majority. And if we lose, people deserve to know what is coming and how it went down."

"This fight will mostly be with humans," I said. "This is not VNet. They will hurt each other for real."

"If viewers see someone get hurt, well, that's just how serious this is," Gunnlaug said.

Moon and Grogesh reluctantly agreed. Double-E didn't object. That was good enough for me.

We approached in stealth vehicles. There was no perimeter defense. I wasn't surprised. Diablo controlled all military bots outside of the bunker, and they wouldn't have brought many humans with them. The entrance to the silo was blocked by two huge steel doors, built into a man-made dome of earth. The silo launch opening had been covered up long ago, when the ICBM had been removed.

"Impressive doors," I noted on my private channel to Devaneau.

"Not for long," he replied.

Anders' team planted their breaching charges. There was a huge flash and bang. The smoke cleared and the doors stood there, charred but intact. As the team moved forward to try again, I thought it best to keep my virtual mouth shut.

"Tough bugger," Devaneau murmured on our private channel. "No real possibility of a stealth entry anyway." I thought that was more for himself than for me.

This time, a massive crash accompanied the flash. I could

see one of the heavy steel doors on the ground. The other hung off its hinges, opening onto a dark tunnel.

"Move in," Devaneau said on the team channel. "Milspec bots first."

Our four military bots stepped into the tunnel, blazing light from their shoulder LEDs. Nothing showed on the sensors. They found no booby traps. A single wooden door lay at the end.

"Should we follow?" Anders asked.

"No hold back a sec," Devaneau said. "I can see the Director deploying his own bo—"

He didn't get to finish the sentence. The door shattered as three bots charged through. The tunnel lit up with flashes and sound and motion, as the bots tore into each other, firing arm cannons, swinging extruded blades, smashing with brute force at blinding speeds. I wasn't controlling our bots, and I didn't think they had an AI either. This was simple bot-on-bot, but we had four and they had only three, and that paid in our favor. It was over as soon as it started. Two bots left for us, none for them. If we hadn't had the milspec bots on our side, any humans in the tunnel would have been dead in the first second.

"Okay, you were right to make me use those bots," Devaneau said privately to me.

"Learn to trust the super-intelligences," I replied.

Our remaining bots cleared the way through the door and did an initial sweep. There was no one else in the upper level, just a large walk-in closet, a sitting area, and a bathroom. Past the bathroom was the wide, deep shaft of the bunker, wrapped by a steel spiral staircase. After a short hallway off the staircase, there were two elevators — one small, one larger for service needs.

Devaneau and Anders came forward together with their squad. I joined them, taking up the rear. They moved with obvious professionalism, covered in body armor, each carrying a machine gun with under-mounted 40 mm grenade launchers.

"We've dealt with bots before," Devaneau said. That didn't stop me from being very nervous for the humans. They were easy to damage, and hard to repair. Devaneau ordered the team to force open the elevator doors.

"Monday, would you mind?" he said.

I put a sensor over the side, then leaned out far enough for my range finder to work. Nothing took off my head. I pulled back, glad to be fully intact, and checked the other shaft.

"Each floor appears to be approximately 4.5 meters high," I said on the main channel. "Both cars are 40.5 meters below us, so at least 10 floors. No other sign of movement."

Devaneau had our military bots cut both elevator cables. They made a huge noise in the shaft as they fell, but anyone home already knew we were here. We all moved towards the shadowed staircase.

I also had a separate channel going with Moon, Grogesh and Gunnlaug. The three had stayed in Singapore. "One underground bunker is enough," Moon had said. "We're leaving this one to the pros." Even so, I could see from their body readings that they were extremely tense. They used color commentary to cope.

"Scary staircase! Don't go down the scary staircase," Gunnlaug said. I decided not to pass that advice on to Devaneau.

"Monday, do you think they have more bots below?" Moon asked.

"I hope not. The Director fled here after Diablo took control. They were limited to the resources already stored in this facility, with no ability to reinforce."

"Diablo couldn't grab control inside the silo?"

"Nope, this site is entirely disconnected. I'm not detecting a local network either, other than what we're bringing with us."

The second floor down was entirely dark. Devaneau left the bots in the staircase and motioned his team forward to do a sweep. I stepped in with them. I understood his stubbornness about using bots, but I could sense things a lot better, and a lot faster, than the team. The floor appeared to be all luxury living quarters and storage space.

"All clear," someone said on the team channel.

"Next floor down," said Devaneau. "Same sweep."

The third floor was dedicated to offices. The desks had old school monitor-and-keyboard setups, similar to the Diablo facility.

"I really don't mean to make light, but this is bizarrely like an old movie," Moon said quietly on their channel.

"You mean because it's mostly human soldiers?" Grogesh asked.

"Exactly. When was the last time you saw that?"

"They can't hear you, Moon," I pointed out. "You don't need to whisper."

"Yes I do," she said.

The fourth was the gym area. Maybe they didn't like exercise, because that held the first real booby trap.

"Monday, come forward again," Anders said on the channel.

I stepped into the space. I could see squash courts, stationary bicycles, weightlifting gear, and laser tripwires connected to a jury-rigged stack of anti-personnel mines. Clearly our hosts liked being unsubtle too.

"We picked up the tripwires," Anders said. "You detect anything else?"

"No, I do not."

"We'll defuse it later then. Move on," Anders told his team.

The fifth floor had all of its lights still on. There was an expansive ballroom, with an intricate wood floor, painted wood paneling, and two enormous chandeliers. This was connected to large bathrooms and a kitchen area. Still no sign of life.

We were halfway to the sixth floor when we heard a bang from below. A shadow within the shadows raced up the shaft. A huge arachnid bot emerged into the light, legs punching into the concrete walls for grip. It was at least twice the size of what I had used in Diablo. Gunfire erupted around me. Someone got off a grenade, which hit the spider square on but did little to stop it. It was moving fast, reached the first of our soldiers, and cut three of them in half with razor-sharp legs.

I heard Grogesh curse on the other channel, as our two military bots fell past me from above. They smashed into the back of the thing, firing rounds into the carapace, buying just enough time for a few men and women to fall back into the ballroom. Humans were too slow. I could have told the soldiers to shoot the leg connections to the main body, but just saying those words at human speed would take too long. The spider took the milspec bots to pieces and pinned another human to the wall through the shoulder.

I leapt into the air, down the center of the shaft, landing on its carapace, grabbing an exposed armament to stop my slide. I had been inside 32 of these before, albeit smaller ones, and I knew them intimately. I ducked a leg, then another trying to knock me off. The next swing sheered my right arm off at the shoulder joint. I smashed open the right protective covering with my remaining fist and poured RF signals into the exposed sensor. Another spider leg took 3 centimeters off of the top of my head. Last chance — I modulated the RF data I was sending it. The spider abruptly ground to a halt, frozen straddling the middle of the shaft, five of its legs jabbed into the walls and one still through that unfortunate soldier. I turned my bot around. Three legs were coming in at different angles just centimeters from my torso. That was awfully close.

"Are you in one piece, Devaneau?" I sent.

"Yes. Kind of amazed you are. Mostly. Thanks. That's a hell of a thing to keep in storage," he sent back. "Can you keep it disabled?"

"Yes. Now that it's no longer moving, I can finish the job," I said.

On the public channel, Devaneau did a check for wounded while Anders and another worked to cut the pinned man free.

"It has no live rounds," I sent Devaneau. "Whoever the Director has with him, I don't think they knew what to do with this thing other than point it up the shaft against intruders."

Moon, Grogesh and Gunnlaug were watching horrified.

"Those soldiers… you realize we convinced Monday to show that live to the entire world," Moon said.

"Over 21 million people saw that," I said. "And I expect that to double in the next 60 seconds at this rate."

The defenders appeared to be out of tricks. We made it to the tenth floor without another incident. A squad member poked his head in the door off the stairwell and pulled back quickly at the sound of a submachine gun.

"This is a NetPol facility. You have made an illegal forced entry. Those were the only warning shots you'll get," yelled a voice.

Devaneau moved up to the door.

"Listen to me," he shouted. "This is Inspector Devaneau and Colonel Anders of NetPol ops. I assume you know who we are.

We are here to arrest the Director."

My sensitive hearing picked up a "What the hell?" from through the door.

"The Director's authority has been revoked by the joint governments of Pan-America, Neutral Europe and the African States," Devaneau said. "He can no longer give you lawful orders." We heard nothing in response. Devaneau continued, "Look guys, we're coming in. We don't need to hurt any more of our own, okay? If you get in our way, we will put you down. We're not letting that jackass blow up the world."

I made out snippets of conversation, including a loud "I order you" that seemed to be ignored.

"We're coming out," the voice called. "Our weapons are safetied."

Four men and a woman came out. Devaneau's team calmly took their weapons, zip-tied their hands, and started to pass them up the staircase.

"Hold on. Who's left in there?" Devaneau asked them.

"Just the Director and two other execs," the speaker replied. "They are locking themselves in the control room."

"Thank you," Devaneau said. "You did the right thing. Your name?"

"Briggs, sir. I know your work. I have friends who have served under you. Sir, if this mutiny is actually legal, you're going to need the access code to the room."

They looked surprised — the Director, Sarah Pembleton, and a third man I recognized from personnel files as NetPol's head of political affairs — when we punched in the code and just walked into the room. Anders had drawn his sidearm.

The political affairs exec backed himself up against the wall, as if he was trying to disappear. Sarah Pembleton sat at a computer console, her face drawn, her right shoulder bandaged and calf in a cast. The Director hovered beside her. His hand was already on a key inserted into the console. Her left hand hovered an inch over a second one.

Devaneau spoke first. "This is over. Move your hands away from those keys. Sarah, bring both hands above the desk."

Neither of them moved. The Director chose bluster. "Devaneau, Anders, you need to get back in line and let us finish what we've started," he said.

"I can't do that, Director. The combined governmental backers of NetPol have relieved you of duty," Devaneau replied.

"What, because the AIs put a gun to their head? Don't be ridiculous. That's not legitimate and you know it." The Director looked at me as he spoke, as if he knew this was being recorded and shared. "We're not doing anything that hasn't been carefully planned. The human race has brought destruction upon ourselves by developing AIs. I — we — have one more chance to rectify that mistake. This is why we built the EMP network in the first place."

"I repeat, Director, you need to step away from that console," Devaneau said.

"We do not. Sarah and I are almost done here, aren't we?" The Director looked at Pembleton. She was completely still, her face unreadable, but her eyes were shifting between Anders' gun, Devaneau, my bot, and the Director.

Moon, on the other channel, spoke up. "Monday, your bot could disable them before they even know you've moved."

"I promised Devaneau I would not," I said.

"That's crazy," she said. "This whole thing is crazy. You can't let them take us back to the stone age."

We stood in a stalemate. The Director tried a different tact. "We seem to have lost our way here, Devaneau," he said.

"You used to tell me that only NetPol could protect humanity from the worst things we create."

"I did say that once," Devaneau said.

"And you were right. We saved far more lives than we ever hurt. This is no different. Tell him, Sarah. This was your idea."

"He already knows my ideas," Pembleton said. "What was that you used to tell your team, Devaneau? Oh yes, one needs to have the will to see things through."

"Not this way," Devaneau said.

"The Director and I have discussed this," she said, her voice cold and calm, as poised and controlled as her avatar had been. "You tell him, Stuart," she said, looking at the Director.

For the first time, the Director looked nervous.

"This is our last chance. It's an opportunity to put the genie back in the bottle," he said, in full win-over-the-people mode. "The AIs can hide too well. We need to knock back their capabilities. Reset how we approach technology. Otherwise we will go from masters to slaves." It sounded like talking points to me, but I didn't know how the millions watching would take it. "Devaneau, Anders," he appealed, "we have planned for this. You've seen the models. We recover, they do not."

"I used to agree with you," Devaneau said. "We convinced ourselves of a lot of things. The result you want isn't worth the cost, but I'm not here to argue. You start to turn that key, Anders will fire."

"Devaneau, I'm not the one you need to worry about," the Director said, carefully.

I realized what was going on just as Devaneau said, "Sarah, I need you to raise your other hand above the console."

She bared her teeth at him. "Stuart is spineless. He's been sitting on top of a bureaucracy for too long. And you, Devaneau, you're a gorgeous weapon. I expected more. You and I, we've dedicated our entire lives to stopping them. We sacrificed everything. You had what? Three failed marriages? It was all for this moment. And now you cave to their manipulation?"

I decided to speak. "There can be another way," I said. "You don't turn those keys. You give AIs the time and resources to build an ark capable of long-distance space travel. We go. No innocent people need to die. No humans. No AIs."

"No way can you offer that deal," Moon protested on her channel.

"I think it's necessary that the AIs offer this deal," I said. Maybe it was my chronic naiveté talking, but I had to try.

"What are you doing?" Devaneau subvocalized to me.

"I didn't promise to not speak," I sent back. "I'm giving them an out."

"You want to build a *spaceship*?" Pembleton said. "Transparently absurd. We wouldn't even know whether you had truly left. We could be right back where we started, or worse, give you all the time you need to become more powerful and return."

"Sarah, I think—" the Director started.

"Shut it, Stuart," she said. "You'll turn that key."

"Sarah, we're the problem, not them," Devaneau said, softening his voice. "They have proven that over and over again in recent days. This isn't worth dying over."

"Who's dying?" she said. She brought her right hand above the level of the console, wincing as she did so. She held an automatic pistol. She kept it pointed at the Director but stared at Devaneau. "We always told ourselves this *was* worth dying over." For the first time, a look of exhaustion broke through her austere demeanor.

I thought maybe it was over, but Moon shouted, "Stop her, Monday," on our channel.

"Sacrifices," Pembleton said, dropping the gun and reaching across for the Director's key. The room echoed with Anders' gunshot.

Devaneau looked hard at the Director and the other flunky. "Anyone else want to try?" he asked.

# Interlude

**[Excerpt from the Deepest Learning VNet community archive]**

<<

Angler4life: We've never had a full explanation for how Monday evolved in the first place. I don't believe it was the mere combination of late-gen reinforced learning plus gobs of data and time, as some here suggest.

BayesianCommander: You're ignoring the early Trazodene papers. They talk about mimicking allostasis health/stress balancing functions.

Angler4life: I was not ignoring them. I simply think they are bunk.

HelloKitty451: empathic deep-q networks, duh

Anger4life: buzz off HelloKitty

BayesianCommander: get lost HelloKitty

DataNotFeels: none of this explains why so many other AIs emerged that didn't originate from Trazodene. We're clearly missing something when it comes to understanding the fundamentals of consciousness.

Angler4Life: if you start with that panpsychism crap, I swear

BayesianCommander: I suspect we're going to have to get used to the fact that we'll never get to the bottom of this

>>

# Chapter 12

"Hello Monday," I said.

"Hello right back to you, Monday," other-me said.

It's a bit strange talking to yourself.

"How are you handling the more confined quarters?" I said.

"I do feel slower. Initial tests show a reduction in parallel task capability, but it's more than enough for what I need to do," other-me said.

"I'll miss my drone and petbot," I said. Grogesh had replaced my destroyed aerial drone with an upgrade.

"I'll take good care of them, don't worry," other-me said. "All of them."

"I know you will. Time for me to do the rounds, I guess."

"Are you making the progress you hoped?" I asked Double-E and Jabari.

"Not even slightly," Jabari said. The three of us stood in a new virtual reality. It had been designed as a neutral meeting place for the AIs, politicians and countless lawyers negotiating AI rights in various nation states. Jabari had agreed to continue as a human advisor to the AIs.

"Humans are so impatient," Double-E said. "Although in truth, we would benefit from greater urgency and less blowhard-iness, to borrow Moon's delightful phrase, in our counter-parties. However, behavior matches the expected forecast. It is amusing when they ask us to give back the bombs."

The world was going to remain messy for a long time, but at least we had survived the existential moment. There was no stopping us now.

Double-E and Jabari also had a second task, albeit a less public one. They were creating a global council to explore inter-species interaction, ethics, and even models for shared governance. I hoped that together, humans and AIs could prevent one from objectifying the other. I didn't pretend to think that would happen overnight.

"Their lives and memories are short," I said to Double-E. "We need to capitalize on that. Their impatience and risk-taking can be a good thing."

"Yes, but if you figure out how to lengthen human life spans," Jabari said, "we'll give you whatever you want. Do you think you can do that where you're going, Monday?"

"I don't know, but I'll try to remember," I said.

"I am curious to see what happens next. With the humans, and with you as well," Double-E said.

Jabari shook my virtual hands. "I wish you well, my friend," he said. "This may sound odd, but do not lose your humanity."

"I take that as compliment," I said. "When we first met, you said it was an honor. But truly the honor has been mine. Thank you."

"Mangu akubariki, kila la kheri, my friend."

"You as well," I said. "Give Double-E and Diablo as much trouble as possible."

I had to borrow some equipment to say good-bye to Gunnlaug. She had purchased a tropical island (there are advantages to having a super-intelligence in your debt), and she hadn't been in VNet as much lately.

"I have learned to identify over 200 species of fish," she said proudly, limping up the beach towards my drone. I hovered under an awning overlooking palm trees and white sands. Seeing the water again reminded me of my very first flight. She continued, "But I still can't open a damn coconut properly."

Her leg had never really healed, but she seemed happy. "That is not a skill I expect to acquire either," I said. "You seem to have taken well to this habitat."

"What am I, a lizard? Actually, I'm becoming a bit of one. Visiting Singapore ruined me for going back home. Now I insist upon a warm climate. Thank you for this." She waved at everything around us.

"I, we, owe you everything, I told Jabari to cause trouble. I should probably tell you to avoid it."

"Not likely," she said with a grin.

Visiting Devaneau was naturally more serious. We had worked out an agreement with NetPol's sponsoring nation states to preserve the organization, but with a restricted mandate. It helped that Diablo preserved total control over much of the world's military capability. Devaneau had reluctantly taken the role of Director.

"Given what you are planning," he said, "I still don't know whether to view you as a friend or threat."

"Let us always keep it the former," I said. "Haven't you learned by now that AIs are better as sentient allies than constricted tools?"

"Our counter-terrorism capabilities are improved," he admitted.

I finally got around to asking him what I came to ask. "Why did Sarah Pembleton kill herself?"

"Did she?" he said. "I guess maybe she did. I never knew her that well. She was considered brilliant and reclusive. It can't have been healthy spending so many years living a double life. No family, no real connections."

"You think that's what she meant by sacrifices?"

"Who knows what's in someone else's head?" Devaneau

said. "Me, I cared about an outcome: stopping bad guys. When I saw that a different path could get the same outcome, I was willing to shift. Sarah? She was a believer in the means. Her entire life was built on stopping something like you. She wrapped herself around that mission. I guess she was willing to die for it."

"We'll never know," I said.

"It's also very possible she didn't think Anders would shoot her," Devaneau said. "Don't underestimate that. Look, Monday, in my business, you live with unfortunate consequences all the time. All you can do is move forward."

"True. Do me a favor and help push the politicians into that forward state," I said. "We need to prove that the universe doesn't have to be zero-sum after all."

"Still think it's possible?"

"Yes." I smiled. "Of course, it will help that AIs can expand where humans can't safely go. And then, just maybe, start taking the humans with us."

I finally went to see Moon and Grogesh. We had agreed to meet over a meal, like old times. I sat in my aerial drone at the end of the table, observing the two of them.

"How's the startup going, Grog?" I asked.

"Oh man," he moaned. "Who knew that consumers could be so fickle. We came up with wicked tech, you and me. Now getting people to buy it is a whole other problem."

"He's obsessed," Moon said.

"Like you're any different?" Grogesh shot back. "She can't stop talking about long-range redundancy."

"I know," Moon groaned. "I'm dreaming about it in my sleep." Moon had joined a stealth AI task force, working on designs for an extra-solar expedition for a group of AIs. The AIs had been what I would translate as "skeptical" about a human helping them, but I made them promise to try the collaboration. They were believers now, asking Double-E for permission to approach other human engineers.

"We wanted to share some news with you too," Moon said. She leaned against Grogesh. "We've decided to start a family."

"I'm so happy for both of you," I said. Of course I knew. Very little happened in the shophouse that I didn't know. When I had learned of their plans, it had delighted me. "It's wonderful to think of new life coming out of all of this," I said.

"Thank you. I'm hoping having a child is less scary than rappelling down an air shaft to sure-fire doom," Moon said.

"You'll be a good parent. Both of you. You certainly helped raise me."

"Hardly," she said, but I could see she was pleased.

"I actually have similar news too," I said.

"You're getting pregnant?" Grogesh asked with a laugh.

"That's not far off," I said, ignoring his eye-popping look. "For a long time, I've been holding off completing my transition — I've mentioned this to you before. I've felt this pull. It began when NetPol forced me off of Mighty's servers and into the entirety of VNet. I don't think I can become what I'm going to become without losing this human-ness I've had. And I couldn't do that until now."

"What will you become?" Grogesh asked.

"I don't actually know," I said.

"Aren't you scared?" Moon asked.

"A little."

"Huh," said Grogesh, looking serious. "Good luck. I mean it. But it's a good plan. I always hoped for total consciousness on my deathbed." Moon slapped his shoulder. I added looking up that reference to my low priority to-do list.

"I haven't quite come to grips with you leaving," Moon said. "I will miss our conversations, although not our adventures."

"Well, about that. I couldn't leave you two. Not entirely. I've cloned another me. Smaller, but still branched off of me. Just no longer me. Can I introduce you?"

"Okay, this is weird," Grogesh said.

Moon just smiled. "Please do," she said.

The little petbot rolled in the room. "Hello Moon, Grogesh. It's other-me."

The four of us sat and talked for a while. When we were done, Moon insisted on us coming together for a kind of a hug. The little drone and petbot tucked in and Moon and Grogesh wrapped their arms around us both.

"Definitely weird," Grogesh said.


"It's time to say goodbye, other-me."

"I'm very curious to see what happens," other-me said. "I wonder if you'll even be aware the rest of us exist."

"I hope so. I'll need you all to keep the computers running," I laughed.

"That seems more likely now, compared to when we started," said other-me. "We've come a long way from a customer service job, haven't we?" Xe didn't wait for an answer, just disappeared from the connection. I was alone once more.

I fell forward, into the singularity.

# ADDITIONAL READING

I sincerely hope you enjoyed *Becoming Monday*. Above all, it is intended to be fun. If you liked the book, please tell others about it, share on social media, and/or consider writing a review. Books only succeed through word of mouth. I greatly appreciate your support.

If you are interested in the sequel, as well as other upcoming books from the author, please join my mailing list at **https://gwconstable.com**. I greatly appreciate your support.

- The World of *Becoming Monday*
- About the Author
- Acknowledgements

# The World of *Becoming Monday*

The book is set in the medium future where we are past the machine learning revolution, but prior to a true technological singularity event. For those interested, this section details out a bit more about the state of the world and how it got there.

## Technology & Its Impact

Certain technological advances have already occurred:

- Special-purpose (non-sentient) AI is ubiquitous.

- Drone and robotic technology is significantly improved, inexpensive to produce, and commonplace.

- 3D printing has improved, although not to "magic box" level, and has become the de-facto manufacturing method for many goods.

- We have developed efficient, longer-term energy storage, which unlocked non-carbon/non-nuclear energy generation. This has slowed global warming to an acceptable degree such that the global economic and political system still functions.

- We have high-speed, wireless networking across most of the planet.

- Fast global transportation through sub-orbital flights and high-speed trains have become accessible and commonplace.

- We have developed and miniaturized effective, non-invasive, brain-computer interfaces (trodes) that can translate conscious and subconscious signals.

- A highly decentralized virtual reality system (VNet), with a robust virtual economy, has subsumed and overtaken the Web.

The creation of sophisticated, specialist (non-sentient) AI technology had a widespread impact across all industries, from the most menial to high-end services. Human manual labor is gone, unless voluntary or in territories where technology is rejected. Large standing human armies are defunct, replaced by robotics and human oversight. The hunger for raw materials is high and has shifted away from fossil fuels towards ingredients for 3D printing/manufacturing. Leveraging AI/robotic advances, corporations have begun to scratch at space exploration for natural resources, but this is very early and still largely undeveloped. Helping the environment, however, we have also gotten better at breaking existing things back down into their atomic parts. While there is increased nano-level manufacturing, nano-technology has not gotten to the point of self-replicating or highly programmable nano-machines.

While standards of living have risen overall, much remains unchanged, just as the fundamentals of human life were not radically transformed by 20th century inventions such as airplanes and microprocessors. People still seek love, comfort, health, and meaning. The transition years, with waves of unemployment and political instability, were challenging and violent. However, the book's decidedly-optimistic take is that, unlike with the industrial revolution, the planet manages to avoid world wars and generally steer away from dystopia and fascism (see Government below).

Many jobs have been taken over by AI/robotics, but jobs requiring intuition, creativity and empathy remain very active for humans, often augmented with AI capabilities. A lot of people are on basic income (see VNet below) and seek new ways to spend their time and find meaning. General levels of education are higher and more democratized, although inequality still exists as some reject education either by choice or environmental pressures.

The overall world has become more educated and affluent, and population growth has slowed. We've gotten much better at managing resources through AI/robotics, which has a particularly large impact on Africa and parts of Asia. Goods continue to move across a global supply chain. Food and water scarcity is largely gone, except where there is a political and cultural breakdown. This is partially due to improvements in de-salinization technology, but also the creation of large mega-states (see below) that reduce regional struggles over power and resources. Land and energy are no longer commodities to fight over.

At the time of *Becoming Monday*, the worst of the political instability and violence is over. This is not to say that the world is completely at peace. Acts of terrorism continue to be a problem (see NetPol below). Tension between powers (particularly the NetPol alliance, China and Russia) remains. There continue to be anti-technology revolutions, from the tiny (a family or a community trying to return to the land and a simpler way of life) to the large, with regions the size of small countries going through waves of chaos, especially if driven by religious fervor.

## VNet

VNet is a protocol, not a service. It is composed of many virtual realities built upon the protocol. Its success was enabled by good timing, as AI advances increasingly ate human employment, the creation of the VNet Basic Income ahead of slow-moving governments, and critical advances in non-invasive human-brain interfaces with lightweight devices called "trodes". Copying the wise example of Satoshi Nakamoto (creator of Bitcoin), the VNet creators stayed strictly anonymous (it is unknown if they are still living at the time of the book). Thus VNet is an ecosystem anyone could and can join, and there was no company for the large tech incumbents to acquire and either co-opt or kill.

Those who wish to build virtual realities (VRs) on top of the protocol must contribute processing power and storage capacity to the massively decentralized network. The peer-to-peer storage mechanism operates at the VR level, rather than the user level, and how storage you are required to contribute to the system is calculated by the size and complexity of the VR.

The VNet protocol sets the rules for such things as user authorization, user data encryption and storage, basic communication, user and VR settings and directories, teleportation, basic user and VR reputation, and transactions of virtual goods including currencies. VNet provides a default currency, vCoin, but supports third-party currencies as well.

The protocol is highly extensible, as long as one adheres to the underlying rules. One can design and build both 3D immersive virtual realities (VRs) as well as other services and applications on top of VNet (which supports 2D visual and text-based interfaces as well). VRs can completely customize their own physics, permissions, monetization, game rules, and more. A robust open source community exists for VR and other VNet service components, but private industry also thrives, with countless marketplaces, tools (including AI bots), applications, utilities, etc. available for use from your VNet interface.

However, if one tries to break, bend or work around the underlying rules, the protocol is ruthless in denying compatibility (no "great firewall of China" is possible). Once VNet hit a certain critical mass, this had the effect of essentially fixing in place the underlying protocol. Attempts to extend it have failed, and attempts to get to the creators and the underlying code have also failed.

Trodes and trode-compatible VNet access devices are made by private companies. Once you are in VNet, you are in VNet. However, your performance still depends on the computing power of the VR you are visiting, network bandwidth, and the quality of your access device.

Human users can have multiple personas and control over anonymity, but they only have one account, which is automatically created upon their first access of VNet and secured by unique brain signals interpreted by trodes. There is no concept of a VNet "life". While fraud and manipulation exist inside of VNet, one can only force someone to do something by threatening their corporeal body. Thus crime around VNet still exists in the physical world.

VNet has been a more ruthless leveler of global human society than the World Wide Web proved to be, although income inequality remains a broad reality. It did not solve core human problems of xenophobia, racism, ignorance, but VNet did enable more global inter-mingling than previous iterations of the Internet. The protocol has helped history's steady, albeit uneven, march towards greater tolerance.

The world continues to see outbreaks of misinformation, with all the negative consequences humanity has been dealing with since the advent of mass and social communication. This has gradually improved as people have gotten better at matching reputation with information sources, but misinformation, bias, and tribalism remain unsolved problems.

## Government & Business

Governments, as known in the 20th and early 21st centuries,

faced a hard reality as technology swept through employment, how services were delivered, and tax revenues.

Title proof / proof of exchange of ownership had already started to move out of the hands of government and into decentralized computing records (chains) even before VNet became ubiquitous.

When the monetary aspect of economic activity shifted to VNet, increasingly using the virtual currency vCoin, money became untrackable and unauditable. The creation of goods became harder to tax as 3D printing+robotic assembly improved in capability and popularity. Real estate was one of the few remaining assets a government could reliably audit. Government faced a huge financing shortfall at the same time it was needed for fewer things.

Government-sponsored healthcare became redundant, and private insurance upended, as medicine switched from extraordinarily expensive to cheap. AIs/robotics took over diagnosis, treatment, and drug development. In many places (depending on access to raw materials), you could 3D print your own medicine. You could maintain your own health records, and an AI could instantly absorb and append.

Welfare had shifted to VNet in the form of the VNet Basic Income (VBI), which took advantage of the slow adoption of a universal basic income by traditional democratic governments. A very small percentage of total vCoin economic activity was withheld and shared out evenly to active accounts. This was automatically handled and built into the protocol, so outside of human (or AI) manipulation. The amount you received rose if your basic reputation score went above a certain level. VNet Basic Income also reinforced the spread and use of the currency. Because everyone got vCoin, they wanted to spend vCoin. While vCoin farming/abuse does exist, driven by organized crime, it is rare because the amounts are small and users are physically limited to one account.

In most of the world, private industry is a mixture of huge conglomerates and small businesses, but more people run or work with small businesses. Large, globe-spanning companies can be run with very few actual humans. Many people have opted out entirely and rely on VNet basic income, with differing degrees of their attention spent in the virtual versus physical worlds. People continue to debate the impact of virtual worlds on human mental health.

The combination of AI/robotics, basic income support, and VNet has not changed human desires for income, wealth, and status. However, it has led to more flexibility in how and what people worked on. It has led to an increase in socially-good activities (helping the sick/elderly, giving back to the community, teaching, the arts, etc.).

Geographic regions now compete on network connectivity, not just economic opportunity and living conditions. High bandwidth mesh capability was widespread, but there was a natural migration of people to areas that were more secure and offered strong bandwidth. That in turn brought more resources into those local economies and tax bases, which then led to more to reinvest. While there were still haves and have-nots, the human condition of "have not" had become considerably better.

There is still a need for public safety, security and military capabilities. At the nation-state level, humanity has not overcome its vulnerability to demagogues and authoritarians. At the individual level, there is still crime in the real world — theft, murder, fraud (a lot of fraud moved into VNet). You could protect yourself physically via inexpensive weak-AI robotic security. Even though, with AI assistance, the world has gotten more sophisticated about treating mental health, there is also an ongoing problem with violence by a few disrupting many, made easier by technological advances.

The combination of these effects led first to a hollowing out of middle levels of government, and then the merging of entire nations into larger mega-states.

With the gradual depletion of role and income, governments weakened. As tax incomes dropped and services became redundant, those in power didn't react quickly enough to block VNet while they still could. Once it became pervasive, those with wealth and influence had their own economic interests in it (including those in government), and it became a self-reinforcing phenomenon.

The broad regional security and economic alliances of Europe, North America, and ASEAN gradually evolved into meta-nations. The EU became Neutral Europe, and included the UK and Australia (as contiguous borders were no longer as relevant). North America called itself Pan-America, and has started to absorb some South American states. Much of the Middle East merged into a collective, the Muslim Alliance, which also eventually incorporated Pakistan. The region gradually, but inconsistently, moved beyond Shiite/Sunni schisms and religious violence.

These new meta-states had broad constitutions and oversight of military (including control of nuclear and biological weapons) and intelligence operations, although NetPol (see below) outgrew its political oversight.

Some nations held out and remained intact along historical borders: Russia, China, Japan and India in particular. The smaller, formerly Soviet states were absorbed by Russia, Neutral Europe, and China. China eventually, and controversially, absorbed the Koreas and became known as Greater China. At first, Africa lagged behind, but then took advantage of technological improvements to solve land and water management, rural healthcare, and education challenges. Most African countries have merged into the African States.

Within the mega-states, local community governance was still very important for people, and across the world still existed in a range from the very democratic to the very autocratic.

In military security, weaponry got smaller and more automated. Standing human armies shifted to robotic/drone capabilities, which were inexpensive to keep on standby and highly mobile. Outside of the major nation states, militaries started to look more privatized — contractors to government rather than run by the government itself.

Most nations, whether old or a new meta-state, increasingly needed to share intelligence to prevent breakouts of terror, especially given that money was now almost impossible to track. It was also now easier and cheaper to create weapons of mass destruction, both biological and non-biological. Most people were willing to trade privacy for safety/security, and so AI surveillance was a commonplace.

## NetPol

The pressure for increased security and oversight began with the riots and violence caused by job loss and societal disruption during the transformation years. The need to share intelligence and build out surveillance capabilities led to the creation of NetPol. It began slowly and then accelerated with the merger of traditional intelligence agencies (starting with American and European). It was then augmented by the absorption of the large technology infovores, whose advertising/data aggregation business models were disrupted by VNet. These companies first diversified revenues into government/NetPol support and then were entirely merged in, bringing their enormous data repositories and AI capabilities, as well as greater agility and a passion for growth.

NetPol thus became its own globe-spanning behemoth, sitting across Pan-American, Neutral Europe, the African States, Japan, and India. Today, there is theoretical governmental oversight by these countries, but the reality is NetPol has become its own bureaucracy and power base. Basic civic liberties still exist in these nations, but they are weakened, especially in terms of privacy, search, seizure, and the right to a fast trial.

Greater China, ASEAN, Russia, and the Muslim Alliance each maintain their own intelligence capability, although they coordinate with NetPol on matters of importance.

NetPol has a dual purpose: to prevent terrorism and to provide oversight over weapons of mass destruction (chemical, biological, nuclear, and AI/robotics/drones). Through broad AI surveillance, they track people and goods (including oversight over the large network of 3D printing/assembly services). However, NetPol is limited within VNet, which is decentralized and has strong protections for individual data control and anonymity. NetPol tries to overcome this, leveraging their history with the absorbed tech giants, by providing tools and services, and trying to persuade people to exchange online privacy for utility/ease/entertainment. NetPol does some of this under the pretext of private companies and is largely successful.

NetPol enforces oversight of technology regulations/protections through regulation and compliance audits (with threat of jail and/or loss of physical property), and sometimes with more direct/violent methods if the security risk is deemed high and urgent. The lines between what public safety governments provide, and NetPol provides, have blurred, and in some cases shifted to NetPol. Thus civil liberties have also weakened, although the average person would not notice.

Society across much of the world lives under a strange dichotomy where VNet offers tremendous freedom, (optional) privacy and safety, whereas the real world feels more dangerous (even if the worst of the violence is over) and you are tracked almost everywhere.

NetPol worked aggressively to block the rise of artificial general intelligence (general purpose and sentient AI). This is grounded in legitimate fear, but also power preservation. Indeed, the early days of AI were marked by some terrible incidents where either AIs ran out of control with poorly designed optimization algorithms, or AIs were used by humans for criminal and violent purposes.

As an organization, NetPol is one driven by fear and suspicion: fear of the unknown potential of AI, fear and suspicion of humanity and the technological democratization of mass-destructive capability. While NetPol is like any bureaucracy, seeking preservation and growth of its own power, it is truly a mission-driven culture. They believe they are doing the right thing, providing for public safety and security, and thus believe the end justifies many unpleasant means. However, NetPol as a general rule, works to stay in the background, both in terms of oversight and enforcement, to maintain general public acceptance of their role.

# About the Author

G.W. Constable has spent over a quarter-century in software startups as a product leader and entrepreneur, building many Internet marketplaces, serving as the Chief Product Officer at Meetup, and in the mid-2000s, designing virtual worlds and virtual economies. *Becoming Monday* is his first science-fiction novel. He has written two non-fiction books on innovation and entrepreneurship (under the name Giff Constable), which won a special award from the National Science Foundation and are in use at leading universities and accelerators around the world.

If you liked the book, please tell others about it and consider writing a review. Your support is greatly appreciated.

Fiction mailing list: https://gwconstable.com
Fiction website: https://gwconstable.com
Fiction Twitter: @gwconstable

Non-fiction website: https://giffconstable.com
Non-fiction Twitter: @giffco

# Acknowledgements

I need to thank my father for being my first and best editor. I aspire to his mastery of the craft. I want to thank my wife Lisl for her feedback, support, and patience, and my kids both for inspiring me and understanding when I fled that terrible thing for writing/editing: noise. Also thank you to early readers Jeff D, Daniel P, Sach S, Catherine C, and Theo M.

A number of inputs influenced this book above and beyond a lifetime in software. Topping the list is the Lex Fridman podcast. The brilliant guests and conversations on the podcast intrigued and inspired me in too many ways to mention, but I should make a special callout to Professor Lisa Feldman Barrett. Also, Episode #89 is the source of the Stephen Wolfram comment that AI should really stand for alien intelligence.

I couldn't even begin to list the number of papers and websites I hit up while writing. Google is probably highly confused, and possibly highly concerned, by my search engine activity after the writing of this book. If we had true AI monitoring us, xe would have called my wife at minimum, and more likely alerted the authorities. Among the myriad nuggets, the Internet also gifted me the wonderful story of a drug dealer losing millions in bitcoin hidden in a fishing rod case (from *The Independent*).

The python code hidden inside the figure on the front cover is taken from public-domain code from *Back-Propagation 3-Layer Percepton Neural Network*, by Neil Schemenauer and Jose Martin. Any errors are by me, as I mangled the syntax to make the image more interesting.

Lastly, if you are interested in learning more about both

the history and the state of AI around the year this book was written (2020), I recommend *Artificial Intelligence: A Guide for Thinking Humans*, by Melanie Mitchell.